BUSHWH

"Neither of you has been near Kate," Clooney said. "She's my woman."

"You think so?" Beckett asked. "Maybe she prefers somebody else."

"Maybe she does," Harper said to Beckett. "Me!"

"You? She prefers me!"

Suddenly Harper lunged at Beckett across the fire, sending the frying pan flying. The two men rolled into the dirt, locked together. Clooney, shocked at what was going on, rushed to them and tried to separate them, and suddenly somebody's gun was out and it went off. The sounds of a slug striking flesh and somebody grunting came in quick succession, and then suddenly there was another shot, but not from any of their three guns.

The three men froze and looked around. They saw Mike Rawlings standing with his gun smoking. He was standing over Kate McElroy. Kate was lying on her side on the ground with a hole in her forehead, just a touch of blood oozing from the wound. Rawlings put his foot on her shoulder and rolled her over onto her back.

"Anybody else?" Rawlings asked.

DON'T MISS THESE
ALL-ACTION WESTERN SERIES
FROM THE BERKLEY PUBLISHING GROUP

THE GUNSMITH by J. R. Roberts
Clint Adams was a legend among lawmen, outlaws, and ladies.
They called him . . . the Gunsmith.

LONGARM by Tabor Evans
The popular long-running series about U.S. Deputy Marshal
Long—his life, his loves, his fight for justice.

SLOCUM by Jake Logan
Today's longest-running action Western. John Slocum rides a
deadly trail of hot blood and cold steel.

THE GUNSMITH
179
THE QUEENSVILLE TEMPTRESS

J. R. ROBERTS

J
JOVE BOOKS, NEW YORK

THE QUEENSVILLE TEMPTRESS

A Jove Book / published by arrangement with
the author

PRINTING HISTORY
Jove edition / November 1996

All rights reserved.
Copyright © 1996 by Robert J. Randisi.
This book may not be reproduced in whole
or in part, by mimeograph or any other means,
without permission. For information address:
The Berkley Publishing Group, 200 Madison Avenue,
New York, New York 10016.

The Putnam Berkley World Wide Web site address is
http://www.berkley.com/berkley

ISBN: 0-515-11969-5

A JOVE BOOK®
Jove Books are published by The Berkley Publishing Group,
200 Madison Avenue, New York, New York 10016.
JOVE and the "J" design are trademarks
belonging to Jove Publications, Inc.

PRINTED IN THE UNITED STATES OF AMERICA

10 9 8 7 6 5 4 3 2 1

ONE

Rick Hartman rarely left Labyrinth, Texas, anymore. The last time Clint Adams got him to leave was to take a ride on a gambling train. This time, it was to go to Queensville.

"Where the hell is Queensville?" Hartman had asked when first approached with the idea.

"It's in Nevada," Clint had said.

"And what is it?"

"It's a gambling town."

"A what?"

"A town," Clint said, "founded just for gambling. It's filled with casinos, gaming palaces; there are facilities for boxing and wrestling matches . . . it's supposed to be incredible."

Hartman had nodded and said, "Now that you mention it I think I did hear something about it.''

"Come on, Rick," Clint said. "You hear about everything. Don't tell me you had no plans to go."

"Why should I go?" Hartman asked. "I have all the gambling I need right here." He spread his arms and indicated the interior of his own saloon and gaming house, Rick's Place.

"I know, but this is different," Clint said. "The town's only a month old, and already it's attracted some of the biggest gamblers."

"Oh," Hartman said, "so you want to go there and risk crossing the path of a Ben Thompson?"

"Ben might be there," Clint said, "and we have had our differences in the past . . . but Bat might also be there, and Wyatt, and some other old friends."

Clint leaned on the table at that point, and Hartman had never seen that gleam in his eyes before.

"Just think of the atmosphere," Clint said, "the *pulse* in a place like that. Come on, you like gambling just as much as I do."

"Maybe more," Hartman said, "but I've learned something over the years that you haven't."

"And that is?"

"It's better to be the house," Hartman said, "and it sounds like in Queensville, the whole damned town is the house!"

Well, Hartman still felt he was right, but he'd gone and let Clint talk him into going, anyway, and now as they were riding into town he had to admit that Clint had been right about one thing. The *pulse* was something you could feel, you could even hear it in your head.

"Where'd the name come from, I wonder?" Hartman asked.

Clint shrugged.

"Probably a safe bet it has something to do with cards."

Hartman nodded.

It was midday and the streets of the new town were teeming with people. The buildings were brand-new—so new you could still smell the wood. In some places there were tents, because all of the buildings hadn't yet been erected. One building in particular was impressive, though. It was a place called the Queen of Spades, and it appeared to be a huge saloon and gambling house. Even though it was early, they could hear the music coming from inside.

"It's beautiful," Hartman said, his eyes shining as he stared at it.

"Down, boy," Clint said. "You have your own place, remember?"

"Not like that I don't."

They continued on, looking for a livery stable, making mental notes as to where the hotels were. There were plenty of other gambling establishments around, some of them attached to a hotel, others standing alone, but nothing the size of the Queen of Spades.

Eventually they found a livery stable and surrendered their horses to the care of a liveryman who knew what he was doing. That he had been working with horses for years was evident by the condition of his hands. They were scarred from years of nips and bites, and the little finger of his left hand had been neatly bitten off to the second digit. Clint felt secure in leaving Duke to the man's care.

Walking to the hotel Hartman said, "My ass is killin' me."

"You've got to get into the saddle more often," Clint said.

"Can't think of one good reason why I should."

They walked down Main Street, which was busy with people coming in and out of saloons and casinos, or simply walking along the street. They agreed on a hotel, figuring one was as good as another, and stopped into something called the Lucky Seven Hotel.

The lobby was plush, furnished with sofas and settees. Over the front desk, mounted on the wall, was a huge pair of dice, one displaying five dots, the other two for the classic seven.

"I think I'm going to like this place," Rick said.

TWO

Kate McElroy looked across the table at Dan Clooney as she dealt him a third card. He was showing a six and she guessed that he was hitting on sixteen. It wasn't going to do him much good. She had two closed queens in front of her, and Clooney just wasn't going to make twenty-one to beat her. He wasn't that lucky.

His third card was a three, which made him really happy because it gave him a nineteen.

"I'll stick," he said.

She flipped her cards over and said, "Pay twenty-one."

Clooney shook his head and flipped his cards so everyone watching could see that he'd had nineteen.

"You are the damnedest blackjack dealer," he said to her.

She had to give him credit. As unlucky a cardplayer

5

as he was, he never showed a temper about it. Most men would have complained loudly, some might have called her a cheater, but Clooney seemed to take losing in stride.

He was a handsome, dark-haired man in his thirties, and he had been in Queensville for the past week. He showed up every day to play blackjack at her table. Once or twice she'd catch him staring at her cleavage, and once or twice she take a deep breath or bend over to give him a better look, just to keep him interested. She wanted him to stay around while she was trying to make up her mind whether or not he was the man she was looking for.

So far he had come the closest, but she still wasn't sure. To be sure she was going to have to get closer to him, and she figured that today was probably the day she should do it.

"Just doin' my job, Dan."

People drifted away from the table, and Clooney leaned over the table to whisper to her.

"Well, maybe when you're finished doin' your job we can get together later tonight?"

He'd been asking her the same question the same way every day. It showed a lack of imagination on his part, which was one of the reasons she wasn't sure he was the right one.

"Maybe we can," she said, and now he looked surprised. She knew what he must be thinking. What was different about tonight? Why had she finally agreed?

"When do you finish up?" he asked.

"About one a.m."

"I'll be here."

She smiled at him and said, "I'll be waiting."

He smiled and dropped down off his stool. That was another reason she wasn't sure about him. He was short, under five nine—an inch or so shorter than she was—and short men usually felt like they had something to prove.

Then there was his partner. Half the times he was in the Queen of Spades he was with another fella, a few years younger than him. For what she had planned she'd need more than one man. It was going to be up to the man she picked to supply the others. She wondered how reliable Clooney's partner was.

As he walked away from the table she wished that the perfect man would come walking through the door and sit at her table. She'd been in Queensville a month, dealing blackjack at the Queen of Spades, and she had seen the possibilities after the first week. That meant that for three weeks she'd been looking for the right man, and he hadn't come walking through the door yet. If he didn't come soon she was going to have to make do with Dan Clooney.

As Dan Clooney left the Queen of Spades he thought that the days of losing had finally been worth it. Tonight he'd get what he wanted from Kate McElroy, what he'd been trying to get all week.

He didn't usually have to work this hard with a woman, but this one would be worth it. She was beautiful, and she was a gambler. He was handsome—he knew that very well—and he was a gambler, and a lot more. They were made for each other.

He wondered for a moment where his partner, Mike

Rawlings, was, but that didn't take much thinking. Rawlings spent half his time at the Queen of Spades and the other half at one of Queensville's three whorehouses. That's where he'd be now, at one of them.

Clooney didn't mind paying for whores when there was nothing else available, but no whore could live up to Kate McElroy. He knew that just by looking at her.

Clooney decided that he'd take a bath before tonight. If she was worth losing all that money, then she was certainly worth taking a bath.

Mike Rawlings looked out the window and saw his partner crossing the street. He shook his head. Clooney was crazy about that blackjack dealer, but she wasn't going to give him a tumble. The sooner he realized that the better off he was going to be.

"M-i-i-k-e?"

He turned at the sound of her voice calling to him plaintively. The whore's name was Fancy. She had a mass of black hair that went wild when they were having sex, and big, round breasts with dark, heavy nipples that he loved to bite and suck. Rawlings had been through most of the girls in the three whorehouses in town, and had finally settled on Fancy as his favorite.

"I'm cold," she said, extending her arms to him, "come warm me up."

He was naked, and as he looked at her his penis hardened. She was also naked, and the sheet was down around her hips. He grinned. She wasn't just cold, she was cold for *him*, and no sheet or blanket could heat up that kind of cold.

"I'm comin', darlin'," he said, walking to the bed, "I'm comin'."

THREE

Clint and Hartman each got a room in the Lucky Seven Hotel and dropped their gear off before meeting in the lobby.

"Where to?" Hartman asked.

"I'd like to go to the Queen of Spades eventually," Clint said, "but first I'd like to take a look around town."

"You do that and tell me all about it," Hartman said, "when we meet at the Queen of Spades."

Clint was not surprised that his friend wanted to go there first.

"All right," Clint said. "When should we meet?"

"It doesn't matter," Hartman said. "I'll be there the whole time, so whenever you're done with your sight-seeing, I'll see you there."

"All right," Clint said, "see you there." They went their separate ways.

Being who he was, Clint had an obligation Rick Hartman didn't, and that was to check in with the local law. He found the sheriff's office, knocked, and entered. The office was twice the size of any he'd ever seen. The gun racks on the walls could have outfitted a batallion. Through a door at the back he could see the cells didn't have the regular type of bars, but a grid pattern.

"Help ya?" the man behind the desk asked.

He was in his thirties, and his clothes looked clean and new. His hair was neatly trimmed, as was his mustache. Brand-new town, brand-new sheriff.

"Are you the sheriff?" he asked.

"That's right," the man said. "Name's Brandon, Ray Brandon."

"Sheriff Brandon," Clint said. "I only just arrived in town and thought I'd let you know."

"Any special reason you're bein' so obligin'?" Brandon asked.

"My name's Clint Adams."

He could see that the man recognized the name.

"I see," Brandon said. "Any special reason you're here, Mr. Adams?"

"It's a new town," Clint said. "I'm here to see it."

"You and a helluva lot of other people," Brandon said. "Course, you're about the only one who bothered to stop and introduce yourself."

"It sounds like a big job," Clint said. "Have you got deputies?"

Brandon nodded and said, "Four, but I could use more. You interested?"

"No," Clint said, and laughed, "not me. I'm just here for a few days to see what's going on, and then I'll be on my way."

"Wish I could say the same for some of the others," Brandon said. "Where are you stayin'?"

"Lucky Seven."

The man nodded.

"Well, I appreciate you comin' in, Mr. Adams."

"It's just a courtesy, Sheriff," Clint said. "Doesn't take much effort."

"What's your game?"

"Excuse me?"

"Queensville's got just about every game of chance available," Brandon said. "I was just wondering what yours was."

"Oh," Clint said. For a moment he hadn't realized that the sheriff was talking about games of chance when he asked what Clint's "game" was.

"Poker," he said. "I like poker."

Brandon nodded.

"Plenty of that available," he said. "Well, enjoy your stay, and I hope you can manage to avoid trouble."

"Well," Clint said, "I always try my best, Sheriff."

"I guess that's all I can ask," the lawman said fatalistically.

Clint left, wondering how a man so young and inexperienced had ended up with the job of sheriff. It seemed to him what a town like this needed was an experienced hand. It wasn't hard to predict what kind of trouble a new town like this was going to attract. He didn't know whose idea it was to build a town around gambling, but they should have put a little more thought into their local law.

FOUR

The town of Queensville had been built by two men, Kyle Merchant and Robert Crays. Both men had been gambling for many years. In the case of Merchant, he had been gambling since the age of eleven, and he was now fifty-one. Crays was almost a dozen years younger.

After an all-night, high-stakes poker game in San Francisco the previous year they had concocted the idea of a town built for and run on gambling. It had taken almost a year to raise the money from many different investors, but they had finally done it, and Queensville was born.

Neither Merchant nor Crays had taken any permanent positions of authority in the town. Although they both sat on the town's board, other people held the office of mayor, the position of bank manager, and other such jobs.

The mayor was a former California state senator named Aaron Sandler, who was in his sixties. His political career was in a state of disarray, and he had no hopes of any legitimate political office, so when they offered him the job he took it.

The bank manager was a man known to both men as a talented con man who had decided to go straight a few years ago. In his own way William Conway—also known to some people as ''Billy Con''—was as honest as they came. Once committed to a job, he tended to follow through no matter what. When he agreed to take on the job of managing the Bank of Queensville, Crays and Merchant knew they could trust him.

As Clint Adams left the office of the sheriff there was a meeting of the town board going on in the town's only brick building. In attendance were Merchant, Crays, Mayor Sandler, William Conway, and three other board members. The subject of the meeting was the first month of existence of the town of Queensville.

One of the other board members was the town treasurer, Calvin Hooper. Hooper had been hired at Merchant's recommendation. He was a former accountant who had lost his Philadelphia practice when he got caught skimming money from his clients to pay off gambling debts. Merchant assured Crays that Hooper's gambling days were over, and that he'd be reliable.

''Isn't hiring him to handle Queensville's finances a little like hiring an alcoholic to be a bartender?'' Crays had asked.

''Exactly,'' Merchant had replied, as if that explained everything.

Crays decided to trust his partner's judgment. Doing so had never failed them yet.

"Let's talk about money," Merchant said.

The board meetings were run by Merchant by unspoken agreement. Crays preferred it that way, and the other members of the board knew they only had their jobs because of these two men.

"We're just about breaking even," Hooper said.

"Even?" Crays asked. "How can that be? Every hall in town is packed every night."

Hooper, a tall, thin, pop-eyed man, stared at Crays calmly.

"You want to look at the books?"

"No, he doesn't want to look at the books, Calvin," Merchant said. "He's just asking a simple question. Give him the courtesy of a simple answer."

"Sure," Hooper said, but when he spoke it was to the group, not to Crays.

"We're not running smoothly yet," he said. "That means that we haven't got the hang of the disbursements. I expect things will improve at the end of next month. We just have to get into a routine, and we haven't had time to establish one yet. Mr. Crays is right, business is booming. We'll have the hang of it by next month."

"Okay, good," Merchant said. "Anybody have any other business?"

Nobody replied.

"Billy?"

"The bank's doin' fine," Conway said, and that was it.

"Okay. Mayor?"

"I have no questions."

"I have one."

The speaker was the seventh member of the board. His name was Ben Thompson, known throughout the West as a gambler and gunman. When Crays and Merchant founded Queensville they realized that there would have to be one huge gambling hall to be the jewel that the town was built around. Having decided that, they needed someone good enough and tough enough to run it. They approached both Bat Masterson and Luke Short with the job, but neither man longed to own his own gambling palace, let alone run someone else's.

The third man they approached with the job was Thompson, and he accepted. In the past month, however, he had become difficult to deal with, and both men were starting to wonder if they were going to have to do something about getting rid of him.

"What is it, Ben?" Merchant asked, while the others looked on nervously.

"My cut's too high."

Every gambling house had to cut their night's profits and deposit it in a separate account at the bank. It was from this account that the town's treasury was formed.

"Ben," Merchant said, "we've gone over this before."

"My cut is still too high," Thompson said.

Merchant shook his head and looked at Crays. Between the two of them they knew that hiring Thompson was Crays's idea. Merchant generally left the handling of Ben Thompson to his partner.

"Ben," Crays said, "we'll have Hooper run the numbers again and see what he comes up with. We'll talk about this again at next month's meeting. Just give us time to get the town up and running, all right?''

Thompson stared at them for a few moments, then said, ''I'll give it some more time.''

''Thanks, Ben,'' Crays said.

''But not much more.''

''Right.''

''If that's all the business,'' Merchant said, ''the meeting is adjourned until this time next month.''

Everyone but Merchant and Crays got up and filed out the door. The mayor had an office in the building, so he only had to go across the hall. The other men left the building and went back to their own establishments.

Merchant and Crays shared an office on the same floor, but they preferred to stay where they were, at the moment.

When the room was empty and they were alone, they had their own meeting.

FIVE

"Thompson's going to be a problem," Merchant said.

"Just give me some time," Crays said. "If he becomes a problem we'll deal with it, but just give me some time with him."

"I'll probably give you more time than he's going to give us," Merchant said.

"Maybe he'll be so unhappy he'll walk," Crays said.

"Fat chance," Merchant replied. "We gave him a contract, remember?"

"Let's have Perry go over the contract and look for loopholes."

Perry was their attorney, who had an office elsewhere in town. He was on a yearly retainer to the partners, but was free to take on whatever other business he could drum up.

"All right," Merchant said, "but I doubt he'll find any."

"What about the sheriff?" Crays asked.

"What can he do against Thompson?"

"Nothing," Crays said, "but that's not what I meant. I was just questioning you about his job."

"He's only had the job a month."

Ray Brandon was Merchant's choice for sheriff. He felt that a new town needed a young sheriff. Crays had voted for experience, but after they had been turned down by half a dozen men—Bat Masterson, again—he had given in and allowed the hiring of Brandon without protest.

"Give him a chance," Merchant continued.

"Kyle," Crays said, "I've already heard from his deputies."

"About what?"

"He's not pulling his weight," Crays said. "He's making them do all the work."

"Maybe he's just delegating authority."

"Yeah, right."

"Look," Merchant said, "we've got enough problems without looking for one."

"You look," Crays said, "there hasn't been much trouble the first month, but this town is busting at the seams now. Jesus, we already have to think about expanding our boundaries. Why wait for real trouble to start? We need a man who can *keep* it from starting."

"Do you have somebody in mind?"

"Yes."

"Who?"

"I heard that Clint Adams is in town."

"The Gunsmith?"

"Right."

"What's he doing here?"

"He likes to gamble."

"Do you think he'd take the job?"

"Where's the harm in offering it while he's here?" Crays asked.

"Where's he staying?"

"Lucky Seven," Crays said. "I heard from the desk clerk who registered him. He came in with a friend, a fella named Hartman."

"Rick Hartman?"

"I think that's the name. Know him?"

"If it's the same man I do," Merchant said. "Jesus, Bob, he'd be a perfect choice for the Queen of Spades. He's got his own place now, in Labyrinth, Texas, but he's run gambling halls all over the country."

"How come I haven't heard of him?"

"You haven't been at this as long as I have," Merchant said, "and he's been pretty settled in Texas for the past eight or nine years."

"Well," Crays said, "it looks like opportunity is knocking twice, here. How about if I talk to Adams and you talk to Hartman?"

"If Hartman says yes," Merchant said, "we're going to have to deal with Thompson."

"I know."

"And he'll have to know."

"Ahhhh . . . let's talk about that one later, okay? First let's see if he's interested—if they're both interested."

"Okay," Merchant said, "let's do it."

SIX

Rick Hartman was standing at the bar in the Queen of Spades, having a beer and admiring the layout, when Ben Thompson walked in. Hartman recognized Thompson, although he had never met him. He knew, though, that Clint and Thompson were not friends. They weren't enemies either; they just never seemed to be thinking along the same lines.

He watched as Thompson walked through the saloon to a door in the back and then went through. Others watched Thompson, too, because while the man was not of the legendary status of a Hickok, Clint Adams, or Bat Masterson, he was just a notch below them. He drew looks from men and women when he walked by, because he had a reputation not only as a gambler, but as a gunman, and—in the eyes of some—as a killer.

Hartman had seen people look at Clint Adams like

that for years, and he knew he'd never know what that felt like. He also knew he never wanted to.

He started to wonder if he should go looking for Clint to warn him about Thompson when another man walked in, and this one he knew.

The man looked around, spotted him at the bar, and walked over to him.

"Kyle Merchant," Hartman said, sticking out his hand, "guess I don't have to ask what you're doing here."

"Rick," Merchant said, shaking his hand, "it's good to see you. Can we talk?"

"Sure," Hartman said, "what about?"

"Let's sit down."

Hartman laughed.

"I'd like to, but there's not a seat to be had in the house."

Merchant smiled, then turned and signaled for the bartender.

"Yes, Mr. Merchant?"

"Would you bring me and Mr. Hartman here a fresh beer at my table, Les?"

"Yes, sir."

"And in the future Mr. Hartman's money is no good here. Do you understand?"

"Yes, sir. I'll let all the bartenders and the girls know."

"Good."

Merchant looked at Hartman.

"Leave your warm beer on the bar, Rick, and let's go talk."

Impressed, Hartman put his half-finished beer on the bar and followed Kyle Merchant to what was apparently his private table.

SEVEN

Clint found that he could not take a turn around town in one afternoon. It wasn't that it was too big, it was just that there was too much to see, and too many people to get around.

He finally stopped in a café for a cup of coffee. While he was seated there a man walked in, looked around, and then walked to his table.

"Mr. Adams?"

"That's right."

"My name is Robert Crays. May I sit down?"

"Can you give me a reason?"

"I have a proposition for you."

Clint sat back.

"I'm afraid I'll need a little more than that, Mr. Crays."

"My partner, Kyle Merchant, and I founded this

23

town, Mr. Adams. I have a proposition to present to you on behalf of both of us . . . if you will allow me to sit?''

Clint studied the man for a moment, then nodded and said, ''Go ahead, sit.''

Crays sat down, and the waiter came over.

''Can I get you something, Mr. Crays?''

''Just bring another cup, Fred,'' Crays said. ''I'll just have some coffee, if Mr. Adams will share.''

''Bring it,'' Clint said to the waiter. As the waiter hurried off, Clint looked at Crays.

''What's on your mind, Mr. Crays?''

''Queensville is a new town, Mr. Adams.''

''I know that,'' Clint said. ''Piss poor name for a town, too, if you ask me.''

''Well, we kicked a few names around and finally came up with this one. I'm sorry you don't like it.''

''Go ahead with your explanation.''

Crays paused long enough for the waiter to put down an empty cup and fill it, then continued as the man left.

''We tried to fill all of the necessary positions in the town as well as we could, Mr. Adams. Mayor, bank manager, treasurer . . . but there's one job in which we might have made an error in judgment.''

''And which one would that be?''

''The job of sheriff.''

That didn't surprise Clint at all.

''I met your sheriff earlier, Mr. Crays.''

''And what did you think?''

''I wasn't all that impressed.''

''See, we offered the job to other men—among them your friend Bat Masterson.''

Clint could have told the man that Bat would turn them down.

"None of them accepted the job, and we finally settled on Sheriff Brandon. We thought a young, new town should have a new sheriff."

"And you were wrong."

"We failed to take into account the kind of trouble a town like this would attract, especially since gambling is our largest commodity."

"So now you're looking to replace him."

"Yes," Crays said. "When I heard you were in town I talked to my partner and we agreed to offer you the job."

"Well, I'm flattered, Mr. Crays, but I have to say no."

"Uh, we'd pay very well."

"I don't need the money."

"I'm sure we could make the office a marshal instead of a sheriff."

"That doesn't make a difference," Clint said.

"You were a lawman once, if I'm not mistaken."

"You are not mistaken," Clint said, "but that was a long time ago. I don't have any intentions of wearing a badge again."

"Well," Crays said, frowning, "I'm disappointed, naturally."

"I'm sorry to disappoint you, but there are any number of men still out there who you could offer the job to," Clint said. "In fact, I could probably recommend a few."

"Well," Crays said, "that would be helpful. I suppose if we can't have you, having someone you approve of would be the next best thing. Will you be in town for a few days?"

"At least that," Clint said. "I could give the matter some thought and then get back to you."

"That would be fine," Crays said. Clint noticed that the man never touched his coffee.

Crays stood up and said, "I hope you enjoy your stay in town, Mr. Adams. Please let me know if there's anything we can do to make it more pleasant."

"I'll do that," Clint said. "Thank you."

Crays left, still looking disappointed.

When Clint was finished, he called the waiter over to pay his bill.

"You're a friend of Mr. Crays?" the man asked.

"Well, I wouldn't say we were friends. Why?" Clint asked.

"Well . . . if you were his friend, you wouldn't have to pay."

"Mr. Crays doesn't pay for anything in town?"

"Nothing."

"And Mr. Merchant?"

"Nothing."

Clint put his hand in his pocket and said, "I'll pay for my food, thanks."

The waiter accepted the money, looking relieved, and Clint left, heading over to the Queen of Spades to meet up with Rick Hartman.

EIGHT

"What's on your mind, Kyle?" Hartman asked.

"I don't suppose you know this, but my partner and I founded this town."

"You're kidding."

"I'm not," Merchant said. "It was our idea."

"Who's your partner?" Hartman asked. "Do I know him?"

"I don't think so," Merchant said. "His name's Robert Crays."

"Never heard of him."

"That's okay," Merchant said, "he never heard of you, either—but I explained who you were."

"You did? What did you say?"

"I told him about your place in Labyrinth, and that you've run places like it all over the country."

"And this is important because . . . ?"

"We, uh, have a proposition for you."

"A proposition?"

"A job offer."

"What kind of job?"

"What do you think of this place?"

"It's incredible," Hartman said. "But what's the job?"

"This is the job," Merchant said.

Hartman looked around, then looked back at Merchant, still not sure he understood correctly.

"This place?"

"How would you like to run it?"

Hartman looked around again.

"Who's running it now?"

"Is that important?"

"It's Ben Thompson, isn't it?"

Merchant frowned.

"How do you know that?"

"I saw him in here earlier. He went through a door in the back."

"Okay," Merchant said, "we hired Ben, but I think it was a bad choice."

"Why?"

"He's . . . difficult."

"Anybody who knows Ben knows that about him," Hartman said.

"Well, we didn't ask anyone who knew him."

"Neither of you had ever met him?"

"Well, my partner Bob knew him, but not well."

"How do you think Ben is going to feel about being replaced?"

"Not good."

Hartman studied Merchant for a few moments before asking his next question.

"Kyle, did you give him a contract?"

"We did."

"And how do you expect to get out of it?"

"Our lawyer is looking at the contract now."

"And do you think he's going to find a way out?"

"I don't know, Rick . . . but if he does, would you be interested in the job?"

Hartman looked around again. His place in Labyrinth was a tenth the size of this, and yet it was his place. He didn't work for anyone. If he wanted a place like this, he could open it himself—with a few investors.

"No, Kyle," he said finally, "I wouldn't be interested."

"Why not?" Merchant asked. "I thought you'd jump at the chance."

"Well, you thought wrong."

"Again, why not?"

"I've got my own place, Kyle," Hartman said. "I haven't worked for anyone else in years, and I don't plan to go back to it."

"Okay," Merchant said, "what if we gave you a piece of the place? What then?"

Hartman paused then, and Merchant went on, as if he felt he had him hooked.

"We can work out the details, the size of the piece, later. Just tell me you're interested."

Hartman hesitated, thinking it over.

"All I can say at this point, Kyle," he finally said, "is that I won't definitely say no right now."

"That's great."

"I have to think it over."

"That's fine," Merchant said excitedly. "You'll be here a few days, then?"

"At least that."

"Great," Merchant said again. "You won't regret this, Rick."

"I haven't said yes, Kyle."

"I know, I know," Merchant said, "but you will."

"Kyle—"

"I'll talk to you later," Merchant said. "I've got to find my partner. Keep the table. You and your friend can use it."

"Kyle—" Hartman said, but the man was hurrying away.

Merchant went through the door and out, leaving Hartman to ponder the conversation. He looked around the Queen of Spades again, at the painting over the bar of a queen of spades, at all the gaming tables that were filled with people and the beautiful women who were working there, and wondered if he could really leave Labyrinth and come here to own a piece of this.

He was still wondering when Clint Adams appeared at the table.

NINE

"You look like you're lost," Clint said.

"I am," Hartman said, "in thought. Sit down, I've got a lot to tell you."

Clint sat and asked, "How did you find a table? This place is mobbed."

"Turns out I know the man who owns the place," Hartman said. "His name's Kyle Merchant."

Clint was looking around and as he heard Merchant's name he looked at Hartman.

"Don't tell me. He has a partner named Robert Crays."

"How did you know?"

"I just met him," Clint said. "He said he and his partner wanted to offer me a job."

"They offered me a job, too."

"They offered me the sheriff's job," Clint said. "What did they offer you?"

"They want me to run this place."

Clint's eyes widened.

"Whoa, this place?"

Hartman nodded.

"And they'll give me a piece of it."

"Jesus . . ." Clint said. "I turned down my offer. What did you do about yours?"

"I turned it down at first," Hartman said, "but then he threw in the part about giving me a piece and I told him I'd think about it."

"What's there to think about, Rick?" Clint asked. "This is your dream palace."

"Well, I'd be partners with them," Hartman said. "I don't know that I want that."

"When would you get to own a place like this free and clear?" Clint asked. "You'd have to have a group of investors behind you."

"Maybe," Hartman said, "but they'd all be silent, off the premises investors. These two fellas are going to be here all the time."

"Yeah, but still . . ."

"There's one other problem."

"And what's that?"

"There's somebody else running the place now."

"Who?"

"And he has a contract."

"Can it be broken?"

"They're checking into that with their lawyer."

"And who is the man?"

"Somebody you know," Hartman said. "Ben Thompson."

"Ben," Clint said. "He won't bow out easily, not unless he wants to."

"I know."

"Does he want to?"

"That I don't know."

"Why do they want him out?"

"Kyle said he's difficult."

"Surprise, surprise," Clint said. "Anybody who knows Ben knows that."

"That's what I said. I guess they didn't know him well enough to know that."

"Can I give you some advice?"

"Please."

"Stay out of it until they've resolved their troubles with Ben."

"Sounds like good advice."

"Have you seen him around?"

"Once, walking across the room. He went through a door in the back, probably his office."

"Tell me something."

"What?"

"If Ben wasn't involved, would you take it on?"

"If the job was open," Hartman said, "I'd . . . have to think about it. I've built a nice little niche for myself in Labyrinth."

"I know."

"I like it there."

"I know."

"I like my place."

"I know."

They sat quietly for a few moments, and then Hartman looked around, spread his hands, and said, ''But this . . .''

''I know.''

TEN

Clint and Hartman decided to remain at Merchant's table for a while and have a couple more beers before they decided to do any gambling. From where they were seated they had a clear view of one of the blackjack tables, and the woman who was dealing was gorgeous.

"I saw her before," Hartman said, seeing where Clint was looking.

"Have you played?" Clint asked.

"No."

"Nothing?"

"No. I've been watching."

"What have you seen?"

They were talking to each other but were both watching the woman deal.

"It's a really professional operation, Clint," Hartman said. "The dealers are good."

35

"As good as yours?"

Hartman smiled and looked at his friend.

"If I took this job," he said, "I'd bring some of my people with me."

"I thought you might."

"You'd have to change your base of operations to here," Hartman said.

"I don't have a base of operations."

"Well, if you do, it's Labyrinth, and if I leave, you'd have to leave, too."

"Why?"

Hartman looked back at the woman and said, "They'd never put up with you there without me."

"Says you."

They continued to watch the woman, who was wearing a low-cut top, distracting the men from their cards.

"She's good," Clint said. "She uses everything she's got."

"And she's got a lot."

The two men looked at each other.

"You or me?" Hartman asked.

"Me, naturally."

"Why naturally?"

Clint started to get up and said, "Because if you end up running this place you shouldn't get involved with the help."

"But I'm not involved now . . ." Hartman said, but Clint was already on his way to the woman's table.

Hartman decided to watch his friend at work and have another beer. If Clint wasn't able to connect with the woman, then it would be his turn.

•   •   •

Kate McElroy had watched Kyle Merchant sit and talk to a man she had never seen before. After Merchant left, leaving the man at his private table—which, in itself, made the man interesting—another man came and sat with the first one. It was one of the players at her table who told her who the second man was. When she heard the name Clint Adams she became excited. Finally, a man who she knew would be able to pull off what she had in mind. Now all she had to do was get him interested.

Getting him interested in her was not going to be a problem, especially since she could already see that he and the other man were watching her. Getting him interested in her plan, though, that she couldn't be sure of. She'd never heard anything about him to indicate that he *would* be interested, but that didn't mean he wouldn't.

She started to play to him even while she was dealing. She never looked at him, but showed a lot of cleavage when dealing in his direction. Both men were talking, but they were looking at her. Finally, he got up and started walking toward her table. She deliberately looked away, and waited, satisfied that she had succeeded in hooking him. Now—all she had to do was reel him in.

ELEVEN

Clint approached the blackjack table slowly. He knew that the woman had seen him watching her, and he knew that she had been playing to him. Now he knew that she was studiously ignoring him as he approached. He wasn't at all sure that he wanted to play that game now, so he continued on until he reached the bar, confusing both Kate McElroy and Rick Hartman.

Hartman was surprised when Clint didn't stop at the blackjack table. Instead he went to the bar, got two more beers, and brought them back to the table.

"What happened?"

Clint sat back down and passed a fresh beer over to Hartman.

"She's playing games."

"What kind of games?"

"She saw us watching her, and when I started over there she was acting like she didn't see me."

"So?"

"I don't feel like playing games right now."

"But . . . look at her."

"Hey," Clint said, "if you want to play those kinds of games you're welcome to them."

"Maybe I will," Hartman said. "I've got nothing better to do."

"Except make up your mind."

"Well, yeah, that."

Hartman didn't move. He remained seated and sipped his beer.

"Well?"

"Well what?"

"I thought you were going over there."

"Let her stew for a while," Hartman said. "We've got all night."

In a hotel further down Main Street, Dan Clooney entered his room fresh from a bath and found Mike Rawlings lounging on his bed.

"What are you doin' here?" he asked.

Rawlings didn't answer. Instead, he sniffed the air.

"Whoo, somebody smells nice," he said. "What'd you put on, two gallons of bay rum?"

"What's it to you?" Clooney asked.

"You're goin' after that blackjack dealer, ain't you?" Rawlings asked.

"What do you care?"

"You're settin' yourself up for a fall, Dan," Rawlings said, "don't you see that?"

"No, I don't."

"You should do like I do and stick to whores. You'd be better off."

"You can have your whores," Clooney said. "Kate is a real woman."

"Yeah," Rawlings said, "a real woman who ain't gonna let you touch her."

"Get out and let me finish getting dressed, Rawlings," Clooney said.

"Yeah, well," Rawlings said, getting up off the bed, "it's time for me to get out and about, anyway."

"I don't see how you can spend the whole day with a whore. What do they talk about?"

Rawlings grinned and said, "Who talks to them? I got their mouths too busy doin' other things besides talkin'. That's what I pay them to do."

Clooney just stared at his partner, who grinned and left the room, shaking his head. Clooney shook his head and changed into some fresh, clean clothes for his night with Kate McElroy.

TWELVE

Robert Crays and Kyle Merchant met in their shared office to compare notes on the day. Crays went first, relating his conversation with Clint Adams.

"There was no way you could change his mind, Bob?" Merchant asked.

"Like how?"

"More money?"

"He says he doesn't need the money."

Merchant shook his head.

"Having the Gunsmith as sheriff—hell, as marshal—would help this town tremendously in its growth. Did you tell him that?"

"I tried every angle, Kyle." Crays said. "He just wasn't buying. What about you?"

Merchant brightened.

"I think I might have had better luck . . ." he said,

41

and went on to relay his conversation with Rick Hartman.

"Well, at least that sounds promising," Crays said.
"All we have to do is figure out a way to get rid of Ben
Thompson without him killing us."

"I'll talk to Perry in the morning and see if he's found
anything," Merchant said. "He said he was taking the
agreement home with him tonight."

"Well . . ." Crays said, settling his left buttock on top
of the desk. Merchant was seated in the leather chair
behind it. It was generally considered between the two
of them that he was the senior partner. As such, when
they were in the office together, he got to sit behind the
desk. The two men made a perfect partnership, because
there was no jealousy whatsoever between them.

"One out of two doesn't make for a bad day's work,"
he said.

"Let's not count our eggs before they're hatched,
Bob. Hartman hasn't agreed to take the job yet."

"You know," Crays said, "maybe if he does agree
it will change Adams's mind. After all, they are
friends."

"I guess it remains to be seen just how strong their
friendship is," Merchant said.

Clint watched as Rick Hartman finally got up and
walked over to the blackjack table. The woman ignored
him until he sat down and began playing. Clint didn't
know what Hartman was saying to her, but it sure
seemed to be working. She was giving him more attention than any of the other men at the table—so much so
that the others left the table. They must have figured if

she was going to take their money *and* not talk to them, it wasn't worth playing.

Hartman had the table and the woman to himself as the clock approached one.

"So you're friends with Mr. Merchant?" Kate asked.

"What makes you ask that?"

"I saw you sitting with him."

"Ah," Hartman said, "you've been watching me, have you?"

Kate laughed.

"While you and your friend have been watching me. He's the Gunsmith, isn't he?"

"He is."

"And who are you, besides a very charming man?"

"My name is Rick Hartman," he said. "I run a little place in Labyrinth, Texas."

"And what brings you here?"

"Just wanted to see a town that was all about gambling."

"Maybe you'll stay on, now that you've seen it?"

"Who knows?"

Kate frowned.

"Is that what Kyle Merchant was talking to you about?" she asked. "Staying on?"

"I can't really talk about that."

"He and Ben Thompson haven't been getting along," she said. "Is he trying to hire you to take over for Ben?"

"Hit me," he said.

She gave him a card, which was a five. He now had twenty so he said, "I'll stand."

She had sixteen and took a mandatory hit. She got a five, which gave her twenty-one.

"You're incredible."

"Nice of you to say," she said, "especially since I might end up working for you."

"I never said that."

"I can make my own assumptions," she said. "Thompson's a difficult man to work with."

"And for?"

"Oddly enough," she said, "he's the one man I've ever worked for who hasn't tried anything with me."

"Insulted?"

"On the contrary," she said, "I appreciate it."

"What time do you finish up here, Kate?"

"One. Why?"

"I thought maybe we'd get a drink and talk."

Kate was already thinking that Hartman was a better catch than Dan Clooney.

"That could be arranged," she said, just as Clooney came through the doors.

THIRTEEN

Clint saw the man enter and watched him. For some reason he just knew the man was trouble, and he was right. The man was spruced up like he was meeting a woman, and he was heading right for the blackjack table where Rick Hartman was sitting.

Clint pushed his chair back but remained seated, and watched.

"I'm about ready to close my table," Kate said to Hartman. "Why don't you wait for me?"

"I'll do that," he said, and noticed that she was suddenly looking past him. "Is something wrong?"

"No," she said, "nothing I can't handle. Just a cowboy who's been pestering me."

"You probably get a lot of that."

"Yes," she said, "and I'm used to handling it."

45

Hartman figured she was telling him to stay out of it. He liked a woman who wanted to solve her own problems.

He turned in his seat just in time to see the man approach. He was short, probably under five nine, and Hartman could smell the bay rum on him before he reached them. The man was well dressed for a night out, but he was still wearing his worn holster and pistol.

"Are you ready?" the man asked Kate. He was smiling and looked eager. Hartman thought he could read the situation pretty well. Obviously, he had managed to cut in on the man's evening.

"There's been a change of plans, Dan," Kate said. "I can't go with you tonight."

"What?" The man frowned. "Why not?" Hartman half expected him to pout.

"I've, uh, got other plans," Kate said. She pulled a cloth cover over her table and looked at Hartman. "I won't be long."

"All right."

Dan Clooney was still frowning as Kate walked away from the table. When she disappeared from sight, he looked at Hartman.

"Whataya think you're doin'?" he demanded.

Hartman turned and looked at the man.

"Are you talking to me?"

"You know damn well I'm talkin' to you, friend," Clooney said. "Whataya think you're doin'?"

"About what?"

"Whataya mean—"

"I don't understand your question," Hartman said, cutting the man off.

"Whataya, stupid or something?"

Hartman smiled.

"No, you just haven't made yourself very clear. What do I think I'm doing about what?"

"Kate was gonna see me tonight."

"Was she?"

"Yeah, she was."

"Well, she didn't mention that to me," Hartman said. "If that was the case, I guess she's changed her mind. That's a woman's perogative, you know."

"A woman's what?" Clooney was confused, and he didn't like the feeling.

"A woman has the right to change her mind," Hartman said. "That's all I meant."

"You know," Clooney said, as if he had just come up with the perfect solution, "I think you better leave."

"Oh, I don't think so."

"Why not?"

"That would make Kate very disappointed."

"Yeah, well," Clooney said, loudly now, "I don't plan on bein' the one who gets disappointed, so I guess that leaves you."

Hartman looked around and saw that they had become the center of attention.

"Look," he said, leaning closer to Clooney and lowering his own voice, "you're making a scene—"

"I don't care what I'm makin'," Clooney said. "You ain't goin' off with my woman."

Hartman was surprised to see that Kate had reappeared already, wearing a wrap around her shoulders. She was wearing it, however, so that her cleavage still showed.

"I'm not your woman, Dan Clooney," she said firmly.

Clooney also looked surprised at her arrival.

"You was goin' out with me tonight," he said accusingly.

"And now I'm not," she said. "It's as simple as that."

"It ain't *that* simple," Clooney said and grabbed Kate by the arm.

Clint was watching closely, in case his friend needed help. He knew that Hartman wore a gun in a shoulder holster, and that he knew how to use it. As long as his friend only had to deal with one man he decided to stay out of it, but suddenly a second man stepped away from the bar and looked like he was going to join in.

Mike Rawlings had gotten to the Queen of Spades well ahead of his partner, Dan Clooney. He had claimed a place at the bar and watched Kate McElroy deal. When the dandy in the suit sat at her table, he knew that he'd been right about her. His friend was headed for a big disappointment—and he knew the way Dan Clooney reacted when he was disappointed.

Rawlings watched as Clooney approached the table, and when his partner grabbed Kate by the arm he stepped away from the bar.

He didn't think he'd ever been disappointed by a whore. Why couldn't his partner ever take advice?

FOURTEEN

"Trouble, Dan?" Rawlings asked.

Hartman had not seen the man approach from the bar. That annoyed him.

"No trouble, Mike," Clooney said. "The lady just forgot that she had a date with me."

"I didn't forget," Kate said, trying to pull free.

"Your friend is looking at a lot of trouble if he doesn't let the lady's arm go," Hartman said.

"Why are you tryin' to get between my friend and his lady?" Rawlings asked.

Hartman studied the second man. Dressed not nearly as well as the first, he was also wearing a worn pistol and holster.

"I think we're on the verge of having things get out of hand here," Hartman said to the two men. "We're the center of attention."

Rawlings looked around and said, "So we are. Why don't you back off, and me and my friend will leave with the little lady."

"The little lady doesn't want to go with you and your friend," Kate said. She looked at Clooney then and shouted, "Let go of me!"

Hartman risked a look at Clint, who seemed poised to join in but then suddenly sat back down. That was when he detected another presence just behind him.

"Is there a problem, Kate?"

"No problem, Ben," Kate said, staring at Clooney. "This man just got the wrong idea, that's all."

"I didn't get the wrong—"

"This lady works for me, friend," Ben Thompson said. "I'd advise you to take your hand off of her."

From behind him Rawlings nudged Clooney and said something in his ear. Hartman thought he heard him say, "It's Ben Thompson, Dan."

Clooney stiffened and then abruptly removed his hand from Kate's arm, as if she had suddenly become too hot to hold.

"Why don't you boys step over to the bar and have a drink on the house?" Thompson suggested. "Let's let things get back to normal."

"No problem, Ben," Rawlings said. "We'll take the drinks with thanks."

Rawlings took Clooney's left arm in his hand and pulled, leading the man to the bar.

"What about this fella?" Thompson asked Kate.

Hartman turned to look at Ben Thompson.

"This gentleman and I have a previous engagement, Ben," she said.

"Ben Thompson," the man said, extending his hand.

"Rick Hartman," Hartman said, accepting the hand and shaking it briefly. "Thanks for your help."

"I don't like to see customers being hassled in my place," Thompson said. "Where are you from, Mr. Hartman?"

"Labyrinth, Texas."

Thompson studied Hartman briefly.

"It seems to me I might have heard your name along the way."

"You might have," Hartman said. "We're in the same business."

"Ah," Thompson said, "and which business is that?"

"This business," Hartman said, indicating their surroundings.

"You have your own place, then?"

"Yes," Hartman said, "in Texas."

"You wouldn't be trying to hire away my best black-jack dealer, would you, now?"

"I wouldn't," Hartman said. "I don't think I could offer her what she's getting here."

"Well, that's good to know," Thompson said. The man looked past him for a moment and Hartman realized that Ben Thompson had spotted Clint Adams, maybe for the first time.

"Would you excuse me?" Thompson said. "I've just spotted an old friend."

"Of course," Hartman said.

"We were just leaving, anyway," Kate said.

"Have a pleasant evening, then."

"Thanks, Ben," Kate said.

Thompson nodded at Kate and then walked past Hartman toward Clint Adams. Hartman realized that during the entire exchange, as pleasant as Ben Thompson's manner had been, the man had not smiled once.

"Shall we go?" Kate asked.

FIFTEEN

Clint watched as the situation played itself out. There was a lot of tension in the air, but it seemed to dissipate when Ben Thompson made his appearance. He continued to watch and could tell when Thompson spotted him. Suddenly the big man was walking toward him.

"This is Kyle Merchant's table," Thompson said. "You have important friends for somebody who hasn't been in town long."

"Actually, I don't know the man," Clint said, "but my friend does."

"Your friend?"

Clint inclined his head and said, "You just kept him from killing one of your customers."

"Ah," Thompson said, "Mr. Hartman from Texas. That's where I've heard his name before, in connection with you."

53

"Have a beer, Ben?" Clint asked.

"Sure," Thompson said, "but in my place it'll be on me."

Thompson sat down and immediately there was a girl at his elbow. She was a busty blonde, not tall, wearing a low-cut, red sequined dress. Her skin was smooth and very pale, and Clint could see the slight blue outline of veins in certain places.

"Carla," Thompson said, "I'll have a beer and bring my friend a fresh one."

"Yes, sir, Mr. Thompson." The girl gave Clint a long look before heading for the bar.

"What brings you to Queensville, Clint?"

"I heard about the town and thought I'd see what it was like," Clint said. "I also thought I might run into some friends."

Thompson sat back, spread his arms out expansively, and said, "And see? You have."

"I should have guessed you'd be here," Clint said.

"Oh? Why's that?"

"You never miss an opportunity, Ben."

"No, I guess I don't."

"I understand you run this place."

"I have that privilege."

"Has it got your stamp yet?"

"Oh yes," Thompson said, "I set the place up myself. I was hired early enough to do that."

"It looks good," Clint said, "and prosperous."

Carla returned with the two beers. She put one in front of Thompson, then moved to Clint's side of the table. She pressed her hip against his arm as she put his beer down.

"Will there be anything else?" she asked him.

"Not right now, Carla," Thompson answered for Clint. "Maybe later."

"I hope so," she said, and tossed Clint another smile before leaving.

"Pretty girl," Clint said.

"I only hired pretty girls."

"Like that blackjack dealer?"

"You noticed her, eh?"

"How could I help it?"

"She's trouble, that one."

"Then why did you hire her?"

"She's damned good," Thompson said, "she brings the customers in. Every once in a while they get into a fight over her, but nobody's been killed yet."

"Probably because you've been around."

"Well," Thompson said, "it ain't because of the sheriff, I can tell you that."

"I met him."

"I don't know what Merchant and Crays were thinking when they hired him. Have you met them?"

"I met Crays, not Merchant."

Thompson studied Clint for a moment, then said, "Let me guess. He offered you a job."

"He did."

"Which one?"

"Sheriff."

"You're not taking it."

"No."

"I didn't think so."

"Told him I'd make some recommendations, though."

"Well, that's good," Thompson said. "The sooner they replace that pup the better."

"I'd take experience over youth every time."

Thompson drank some beer and regarded Clint curiously.

"So you just came to have a look?"

"Oh," Clint said, "I expected to stay a few days, maybe do some gambling."

"This is the place to do it," Thompson said. "No point in going to any of the other places."

"What do you think of this idea, Ben?"

"You mean the idea of a town built around gambling?" Thompson shook his head. "It'll never work."

"Why not?"

"There's just too much that can go wrong," Thompson said. "You know gamblers, Clint, and most of the trouble won't even come from them. It will come from the men who think they're gamblers."

"The sore losers."

"Exactly . . . like that fella there, with his friend?" Thompson indicated the men Hartman had had his run-in with. "Sore losers are even worse when they come in twos."

Clint was glad to see the two men still standing at the bar. It meant they hadn't followed Hartman and the woman outside.

"Well," Thompson said, "I've got to get back to work. I just saw you sitting here and thought I'd come over and say hello."

"That was nice of you, Ben."

Thompson stood up.

"Anybody else in town I should know about?" Clint asked.

"Not yet," Thompson said, "but I expect some old friends will be showing up anytime, now. You have what you want from the bar, Clint. Your money's no good there, but at the tables . . . well, that's a different story."

"Thanks, Ben."

It was an odd thing, Clint thought. He and Ben Thompson had friends in common—Luke Short being first and foremost, probably—and yet they could never be more than civil to each other. Actually, this was a better reception than he might have expected. Thompson must have been getting mellow in his old age. He was at least as old as Clint.

Clint followed Thompson's progress through the room to a door in the back, which he disappeared through. He looked over at the bar then and saw that the two sore losers were now missing.

"Ah, shit," he said, and got up quickly.

SIXTEEN

Clint went outside. It was dark, with hardly any moon. He looked both ways but couldn't see anything. He doubted that the two men had left in time to follow Hartman and the woman, and neither had he. He had no idea which way they had gone.

Suddenly he heard voices off to the right. He stood still and listened.

"Come on, Dan," a man said, "forget it."

"I don't wanna forget it," Dan said.

Clint knew it was the two men. Apparently the one called Dan was still steaming about losing "his woman."

"Come on," the other man said, "let me show you why whores are the best."

"Why?" Dan asked belligerently.

"They never leave you for somebody else. They're yours for as long as you pay them."

Clint waited to see if the first man would be able to convince Dan of this. Personally, Clint didn't see the need for whores when there were plenty of women around who would sleep with you simply because they wanted to.

"I wanna find 'em," Dan said.

"Well, then, you'll have to look for them alone," the other man said. "It's stupid to get all upset about a woman who doesn't want to be with you."

"I'll show 'er," Dan said, and his voice faded away. The first man came out of the darkness, heading back to the saloon, and stopped short when he saw Clint standing there.

"I think your drunken friend is looking for trouble," Clint said.

"Aw, he ain't drunk," the man said, "he's just stubborn. Your friend any good with a gun?"

"He's a fair hand."

"So's Dan," the man said. "Maybe it'll be an even match."

"If neither one of us rakes a hand it will be," Clint said.

"Oh, you mean like before?" the man said. "I wasn't gonna back Dan's play. I just wanted to keep things quiet. I know Ben Thompson doesn't like gunplay in his place. My name's Rawlings, by the way, Mike Rawlings."

"Clint Adams."

"I know who you are, Adams," Rawlings said, "and I got no beef with you."

"I don't have one with you either."

"Fine," Rawlings said, "then how about letting me buy you a beer?"

Clint studied the man and found himself believing that he was sincere.

"Why not?"

SEVENTEEN

Hartman sat on the bed and watched while Kate undressed. She had taken him to her room and turned up the gaslight on the wall just enough to bathe the room in a yellowish glow. When she was naked it made her body look golden. Her breasts were large and round, with large nipples that stood out more than any he had ever seen. He was absolutely fascinated by them. When she came to him she pressed his face to her breasts, and he explored them with his tongue, taking those long nipples into his mouth. She moaned and wrapped her fingers in his hair, rubbing his face back and forth across her nipples.

She released his head then and dropped to her knees. She began to undress him, and he felt like a present that was being unwrapped. First she unbuttoned his shirt and slid her hands inside, pressing her palms to his flesh.

She slid the shirt down his arms and tossed it away, then undid his belt buckle. She pulled off his boots, and then his trousers as he lifted his hips to help her. Next she slid his underwear down to his ankles and removed them and his socks at the same time.

His erection was standing straight up from between his thighs, and she rocked back on her heels for a moment to gaze at it. Her eyes were shining as she reached for him and ran her nails along the underside of his penis. He caught his breath and leaned back on his hands to watch her.

She touched him gently, then slid her hands onto his thighs and leaned forward. Her tongue flicked out, touching the spongy head of his penis, then she took hold of him with one hand and began to lick him, looking up at him at the same time. The tip of her tongue licked the tender spot underneath his penis, just beneath the head, and she was smiling and looking at him at the same time. Suddenly, she opened her mouth and engulfed him. The sensation was so exquisite that he gasped and held his breath. Then she started to move her head up and down, up and down, slowly at first, moaning as she did so, then faster and faster, until Hartman abruptly grabbed her hair with one hand and pulled her off of him.

"What?" she gasped, her mouth wet and shiny. His penis covered with her saliva, was suddenly cold.

"You've got to go slower if you want this to last," he warned.

"Don't worry," she said. "I'll bring you back again. I promise."

With that she bent to her task again, lovingly taking

him back into her mouth. The heat was even more intense this time, because he'd been so cold seconds before.

"Jesus—" he said, leaning back again and watching her. What was erotic, though, was that he could not only watch her, but he could hear her. She was suckling him noisily, as if he was just so delicious that she was only concerned with devouring him, and not with being quiet about it.

Her head continued to bob up and down in his lap until suddenly he lifted his butt off the bed and exploded into her insistent mouth. . . .

Later she kept her promise. Using her fingers and her tongue and her mouth she brought him back to life, hard as before, and then she sat on him. He was still seated on the edge of the bed. She eased herself down into his lap, taking his penis deep inside of her, and the heat there made the heat of her mouth seem cool.

She locked her hands behind his neck and began to ride him. He reached beneath her to cup her buttocks, which were slick with sweat.

He felt the rush that seemed to be coming up from his ankles and then he was erupting inside of her. She continued to ride him up and down, her vagina tightening on him as if she was milking him for every drop.

She came to a halt then and leaned against him. Their bodies were sticky with sweat and stuck together.

"I hope," she said into his ear, "you don't think we're done."

"Jesus . . ." he said.

It was going to be a hell of a night.

EIGHTEEN

Clint was surprised to find himself liking Mike Rawlings. The man was in his thirties and had very definite opinions about things other than whores, and he wasn't shy about discussing them.

Gambling, for instance. He found no fascination in risking his hard earned money on the turn of a card or the roll of some dice.

"I worked too damn hard for my money," Rawlings said, then added, "that is, when I have any money."

Clint had already heard his opinions on whores, and he found them—as well as many others—to be interesting and well thought out.

Where they differed, though, was on the subject of women.

"The devil put them here," Rawlings said.

"What?"

"It's true," Rawlings said. "You know the story of the Garden of Eden?"

Clint nodded.

"Well, it's wrong," the other man said. "God put Adam there, but the devil put both Eve and the apple there."

"Where did you get an idea like that?" Clint asked.

"Years of watching women," Rawlings said, "and of being watched by them. They're evil, take my word for it."

"I won't," Clint said. "I have my own opinions about women."

"And what are they?" Rawlings asked.

At that moment Carla, the blonde who had brought drinks to the table for Ben Thompson and Clint, passed by, and Clint used her as an example.

"Carla, can you come here for a minute?"

"You remembered my name," she said, pleased.

"How could I forget."

"What can I do for you?" she asked, giving him a suggestive look.

"Just stand here a moment."

"That's it?"

"That's all."

"Well, all right."

Clint pointed at Carla and said, "Carla is a perfect example of what is beautiful about women."

"Whoa," she said, leaning against him.

"Women are lovely creatures, Mike, inside and out."

"I've known some pretty ugly ones, Clint."

"It's the same with men," Clint said. "There are

good and bad on both sides. Look at Carla, talk to her. She's completely delightful.''

''You are making so many points,'' Carla said to Clint.

''Thanks for helping me, Carla. I'm trying to convince my friend that all women aren't created evil.''

She leaned even closer to Clint and said, ''I finish here at three.''

''Don't you have to get to sleep?'' he whispered.

''Sure,'' she said, ''there'll be plenty of time to sleep . . . after?''

He put his hand against her bare back, enjoying the feel of her skin, and said, ''I'll be here.''

She took his hand, squeezed it, and then looked at Mike Rawlings.

''Listen to your friend,'' she said. ''He knows how to treat a woman.''

As Carla walked away, Rawlings said, ''Whores.''

''What?'' Clint asked.

''I said they're all whores,'' Rawlings said, ''and they should be treated that way.''

''This is about the only thing I have to disagree with you on, Mike, but my disagreement is strong.''

''That's okay,'' Rawlings said, ''everybody is entitled to his own opinion. Mine just happens to be that women are the root of evil.''

''Do you ever talk to the whores you're with, Mike?'' Clint asked.

''I don't pay them to talk,'' Rawlings said, recalling that he had said the same thing to Dan Clooney on many occasions.

''Well,'' Clint said, finding that he didn't quite like

the man as much as he had first thought, "I guess I'll try to get a little gambling in before they close the place down."

"Time for me to leave, anyway," Rawlings said.

"Thanks for the beer, Mike."

"Sure, Clint," Rawlings said, "anytime. I'd better go out there and see if Dan is still prowling the streets."

"Good luck."

"You're the one who's gonna need luck," Rawlings said, and left.

Outside, Dan Clooney, who was not drunk because he hadn't had time to get drunk before Kate and Hartman left the saloon, was stumbling around as if he *were* drunk. Goddamn, he thought, I know I didn't have that much to drink, but I feel drunk. He couldn't understand—and probably never would, even if someone had explained it to him—the concept of being drunk with anger.

What he did understand finally, though, was that he was not going to find them tonight. If he was going to do something about getting Kate back—an odd concept, since he'd never quite had her—he was going to have to do it in the morning.

He headed back to his hotel, wondering if using one of Rawlings's whores wasn't just what he needed to take the edge off his anger.

NINETEEN

"I have a plan."

"A plan for what?" Hartman asked Kate.

"To rob the Queen of Spades."

"I have a plan, too."

"For what?"

"To rob the United States Mint."

They were lying in bed in her room, having just finished making love four or five times. Hartman had lost count. The last one had hurt a little bit, so he figured that for five.

Kate McElroy was the most insatiable woman he had ever been with. She managed to bring him fully erect any time she wanted to, and then proceeded to use him for as long as she wanted before *allowing* him to finish. No woman had ever treated him this way and, as much as he had enjoyed the sex, he didn't think he wanted to experience it again. He didn't like the feeling of having absolutely no control over the situation.

And there was another problem. As many times as Kate had satisfied Hartman, he did not seem to be able to offer her the same satisfaction. It was something he did not feel comfortable discussing with her, but he would have liked to have known if this was normal for her, or a failing on his part. He'd been trying to figure out how to ask her this when she announced that she had a plan.

"What if I told you I was serious?"

"Okay," he said, "for the sake of argument, you're serious. What's the plan?"

"I don't want to tell you that unless you're in."

"In what?"

"I need a man to help me."

"Help plan it?"

"No," she said, "I have a plan, but who's going to listen to a woman? I need a man to work with me, and to bring in the other three men I'll need."

"Three more men?"

"The job takes four men," she said, "and me."

"Kate . . . this is crazy talk. You're kidding, right?" he asked.

"Tell me you'll help me and I'll tell you if I'm kidding."

"Kate—"

She reached down and took his penis in her hand.

"Oh, no," he said, "not again."

It was amazing. She slithered down between his legs and used her talented mouth to bring him fully erect again. Then she began to suck him until he was almost ready to explode. She stopped him by wrapping her fingers around the base of his penis and squeezing tightly. After that she took his penis between the thumb, forefinger, and middle finger of her hand and began sliding them up and down the length of him with tantalizing slowness. The exquisite pain/pleasure was almost unbearable. She'd bring him almost to the point of completion, and then stop.

"Jesus," he said at one point, "what are you trying to do to me?"

"Win you over to my side," she said, licking the head of his penis. "Tell me you'll help me and I'll finish you."

"Kate—"

"Mmmm-mmm," she murmured, taking his penis in her mouth and sucking it slowly. She let it slip from her mouth, sucking it one last time between her lips. The organ was prodding the air, begging for release.

"Tell me," she said, sliding her fingers up and down as he swelled even larger than before, "tell me . . . come on, tell me . . ."

"All right, all right, I'll help you," he said.

"That's my baby," she said.

Her mouth descended on him, took him inside, and after a few bobs of her head he ejaculated. She moaned and sucked on him until there was nothing left in him, and then she let him go. She lay down next to him, snuggling up against him.

"We'll sleep now," she said, "and talk more in the morning."

"Jesus," he said, "you mean you do sleep?"

TWENTY

"So she outlines this plan to rob the Queen of Spades," Hartman told Clint the next morning, "and you know what? It would work."

"Come on, Rick," Clint said. "Do you think she was serious?"

"Well, of course not . . . I don't think . . ."

"Because if it was you'd have to tell the sheriff."

"The sheriff you have so much respect for?" Hartman asked sarcastically.

"Well, then, you'd have to warn Ben."

"And tell him what? One of his dealers is planning to rob him, and oh, by the way, it's a woman?"

"So what do you plan to do?"

Hartman thought a moment. They were in a café down the street from their hotel, having breakfast. Clint took advantage of the moment's silence to fork some food into his mouth.

"You know what I think?"

"What?"

"It was part of the sex."

"What?"

"No, I'm serious," Hartman said. "I have never been with a woman to whom control was so important. She just wanted to know that she controlled me, and that I'd agree to anything she wanted so she'd . . . well, you know . . ."

"No," Clint said, enjoying his friend's discomfort, "I don't know."

"Well, if you did know, you'd understand. The woman is insatiable."

"That's not something I've ever heard you complain about before."

"This was different."

"How?"

"Well . . ." Hartman leaned closer. "She never . . . you know, finished."

"Never?"

Hartman shook his head.

"It was probably why she was able to go on and on, because she was never . . . drained, you know? You know how tired women get . . . after?"

"I know how tired most men get . . . after," Clint said, still enjoying his friend's attitude.

"Well . . . this was just really weird."

"Is it an experience you'd like to repeat?" Clint asked.

"No," Hartman said without hesitation.

"Well, I'll tell you something," Clint said, "I wouldn't mind repeating my night . . ."

TWENTY-ONE

Clint had waited around the Queen of Spades until Carla was finished, and then they had gone to his hotel room.

"My room's in the saloon and there wouldn't be much privacy," she explained.

"My room is fine with me, Carla."

She hung on to his arm while they walked to his hotel.

"Can I ask you something?"

"Sure," Clint said. Considering what they were about to do, she was entitled to a few questions.

"Did you mean all those things you said about me? About women, I mean, to your friend?"

"Every word."

"I don't think I ever met a man before who talked like you."

"I'm not so special."

73

"Well," she said, "guess I'll know more if you are or not in a little while."

When they got to his room Carla told him to sit on the bed.

"I'll undress slow for you."

"Okay." Clint enjoyed watching women undress.

Undressing was not a difficult thing for her. She was wearing her saloon dress, which didn't cover that much of her anyway. He knew her breasts were impressive, but when she peeled the dress down slowly and each breast came into view he caught his breath. She was probably in her twenties, and her breasts were beautiful. Round and heavy, with marvelous nipples that seemed to stare at him. Maybe when she was in her late thirties, or her forties, they would sag, but at that moment they were perfect examples of what a woman's breasts should look like.

In his opinion, of course.

When she was naked she said, "Your turn," and she stood there with her hands on her ample hips while he undressed.

When he was naked he said, "Turn around."

"Why?"

"I want to see if your butt is as beautiful as your breasts."

She giggled and turned, sticking her butt out slightly.

"Oh, yes," he said. "It matches up very nicely, doesn't it?"

"Some of the other girls say my butt is too big," she said, turning back to face him.

"Well, Carla," he said, "I think some of the other

girls are jealous. You have got a gorgeous butt.''

"Would you like a closer look?" she asked.

He grinned and said, "I thought you'd never ask."

"Are you daydreaming?" Hartman asked.

"Hmm?" Clint said. "Oh, yeah, I guess I was. I was remembering my night. That Carla—"

"Which one is she?"

"Short blonde with a great figure."

"I think I know which one. Maybe we should switch."

"Why?"

"You like the kind of woman Kate is."

"I like the kind of woman Carla is, too."

"It's not nice to hold out on a friend," Hartman said. "Besides, wouldn't you like to experience Kate after everything I've told you?"

If Rick Hartman knew one thing about his friend it was that he liked a challenge.

"You're a nasty man, Rick."

"Ha," Hartman said, "then you are curious."

"What man wouldn't be?"

"Then you make your play tonight," Hartman said, "and maybe she'll make you the same offer she made me."

"To help her rob the saloon?"

Hartman nodded.

"Rick, the woman can't be serious about that," Clint said, "now can she?"

Hartman took a sip of coffee and said, "I sure hope not."

TWENTY-TWO

Clint woke with Carla's breasts pressed into his back. For a moment he thought she was asleep, but then he felt her hand glide over his thigh and between his legs. By the time her hand reached his penis it was already hardening.

"Oooh," she said, "are you awake?"

He didn't answer.

"Come on," she said, "I know you're awake. This doesn't happen when a man's sleeping." She squeezed his erect penis as she spoke.

"Sure it does," he said.

"It does?"

"Sometimes."

"When you're alone?"

He hesitated, then said, "Sometimes."

"Well . . . what do you do with it when you're alone?" she asked.

He turned to face her, his penis lying flat against her belly.

"Let's not talk about that now. . . ."

"Hey!"

"What?"

"You're daydreaming on me again."

Clint looked across the table at Hartman.

"Sorry."

"Are you thinking about Carla," Hartman asked, "or Kate?"

"Carla," Clint said. "There's no reason to think about Kate . . . yet."

"I'm really curious to see if she makes the same offer to you."

"Speaking of offers," Clint said, "have you decided what you're going to do about yours yet?"

"To tell you the truth," Hartman said, "I haven't really thought much about it."

"I talked to Ben yesterday."

"Oh, that's right," Hartman said. "When we left he was walking over to you. What happened?"

"Not much."

"Were you two . . . civil?"

"Yeah, we were," Clint said, sounding surprised, "more than in the past."

"That's surprising. Did you, uh—you didn't mention about . . ."

"No, I didn't."

''You know,'' Hartman said, ''if I take the job I'll be responsible for him losing his.''

''Is that a fact?'' Clint said. ''I mean, aren't they going to get rid of him anyway?''

''Not if they can't replace him.''

''Why don't they run the place themselves?''

Hartman hesitated, then said, ''I don't know. I didn't ask.''

''Well don't.''

''Why not?''

''It might cost you a job,'' Clint said. ''Wait until you turn it down, then make the suggestion.''

''Good thinking,'' Hartman said. ''What about your decision?''

''What about it? I already made it.''

''Well, would my decision affect yours?''

''In what way?''

''Well . . . if I took the job, would you consider—''

''No,'' Clint said, interrupting him, ''I won't change my mind and put on a badge.''

''Well, what about moving here?''

''Moving here?''

''I mean—I know you don't *live* in Labyrinth, it's just sort of an . . . unofficial base for you, but . . .''

''I know what you mean,'' Clint said. ''I like Labyrinth.''

''I know.''

''It's . . . quiet. That's why I go there. This town . . . well, there's a big difference.''

''I know.''

There were a few moments of awkward silence and then Hartman said, ''Can I ask you something?''

"Sure."

"I need your advice," he said. "What would you do?"

"If I had my own place in Labyrinth," Clint said, "and somebody offered me the Queen of Spades, I'd make sure that the Queen of Spades—and this town—were going to be around for a while."

"And you don't think they will?"

Clint took a moment before he replied.

"I'm not sure that *gambling* is something to build a town on."

"You gamble," Hartman said. "You like it."

"I know," Clint said, "but I'm not a gambler—I mean, not in the sense that Luke Short and Bat Masterson—or even you—are."

"Me?"

"Sure," Clint said. "Opening your own place, that's a gamble, isn't it?"

"I suppose so."

"And so would taking this job be," Clint said. "Sure, it's a bigger place and you'll probably make a lot more money, but how long would it last?"

"Well," Hartman said, "I could take this job and keep my place in Labyrinth going."

"Who'd run it?"

Hartman shrugged.

"One of the bartenders, maybe."

"Sure."

"Maybe one of the girls who have been with me for a while?"

"Sure," Clint said again, "one of them could run it."

"Or you?"

"That's not an option."

"Okay, not you, but there *are* other options, that's the point."

"So all you've got to do is explore them, and make your decision."

"Right."

"How long is that going to take?"

"I don't know."

"Because I only intended to be here for, you know, a few days."

"Well, so did I."

"Do you think you can make a decision in that time?"

"Sure," Hartman said, "sure, I can do that."

"Okay, then good luck. Whatever you decide is all right with me."

"Thanks."

"Just remember one thing."

"What?"

"If you're in," Clint said, "Ben Thompson is out."

"So?"

"You might have to deal with Ben."

Hartman looked down at the remains of his breakfast, lost his appetite, and pushed it away.

TWENTY-THREE

Since their first day in town was so eventful Clint decided to pretty much spend the second day in one place. He decided to take a look at some of the gaming tables in the Queen of Spades.

Poker was his game, but he tried not to play at tables that had house dealers, and all of the tables did, so he started to look elsewhere.

During the course of the day he played some faro and roulette, and spent some time talking to Carla when she came to work.

In fact, he spent some time daydreaming about her as he watched her move around the room. . . .

Clint didn't remember ever having spent so much time on a girl's behind.

"You really like my behind?" she asked, while he was kissing it.

"I worship it," Clint said, running his tongue along the crease between her cheeks, "I adore it. I think it's the world's greatest—"

"Stop talking," she said, "keep licking. . . ."

At different times during the day Clint talked with Ben Thompson, Robert Crays, and—introduced by Crays—Kyle Merchant.

Thompson simply stopped by him while he was having a beer to ask how he was doing.

"I'm even," Clint said. "Your roulette wheel seemed to be honest."

"Really?" Thompson said. "I guess I'll have to look into that."

Later Crays came in with another man when Clint was moving away from the faro table.

"How are you doing?" Crays asked, echoing Thompson.

"Faro's never been my game," Clint said, "and the dealer seems very good."

"I understand you're friends with Wyatt Earp," the other man said. "He's said to be quite a faro dealer."

"He is."

"Clint, this is my partner, Kyle Merchant."

Clint shook hands with the man, who appeared to be in his early fifties.

"We were looking for Rick Hartman," Merchant said. "Is he around?"

"I had breakfast with him," Clint said, "so he didn't leave town, if that's what you mean."

"No, no," Merchant said, "we weren't concerned about that. Did he tell you about our offer?"

"We told each other," Clint said.

"You haven't changed your mind, have you?" Crays asked.

"No, I haven't."

"Well," Merchant said, "then that just leaves his decision. Is he ready to make it yet?"

"I guess you'll have to ask him that," Clint said, "when you find him."

"Of course," Crays said, "we wouldn't try to pressure him."

"Sure you would."

"Well . . ." Merchant said, and the three of them stood there awkwardly.

"Well . . ." Clint said.

"We'd better get going," Crays said. "We've, uh, got other business. . . ."

Clint stood at the bar until they left, then turned and saw Kate McElroy opening her blackjack table. He didn't really know until that moment that he'd been waiting for her.

Carla was cute and had a nice body—a wonderful butt—but Kate was a woman and, from what Hartman had told him, she was interesting.

And he hadn't played blackjack all day.

Crays and Merchant stopped just outside the front doors of the saloon.

"Why don't you keep looking for Hartman," Merchant suggested.

"And what will you be doing?"

"I think I'll go and talk to Perry," Merchant said. "He's had enough time to check over the agreement we signed with Thompson."

"Why should he even have to check it over?" Crays complained. "He's the one who drew it up."

"I know," Merchant said. "That's something else we can learn from this experience."

"What's that?"

"Next time we have an agreement drawn up," Merchant said, "we'd better have a built-in escape clause."

"Maybe we need a new lawyer," Crays said. "You'd think Perry would have known that already."

"He'll do for now," Merchant said. "Once we get this matter cleared up, we can see if we can entice a better man to move here and handle our affairs."

"Maybe somebody from San Francisco or New York."

"We'd have to pay him a lot of money."

"Hopefully," Crays said before they split up, "we'll be making a lot of money."

TWENTY-FOUR

Dan Clooney sat in his room, thinking about the whore he'd been with last night. When he had gotten back to his hotel Rawlings was there, in his own room this time, and he had had the whore, Fancy, with him. Clooney knew this because he knocked on the door and when Rawlings answered he could see the girl on the bed behind him.

"Sorry to interrupt you . . ."

"You didn't do anything stupid, did you, Dan?" Rawlings asked.

"Like what? Oh, you mean about Kate? No. In fact, I was thinkin' you might be right."

"About what?"

Clooney looked past Rawlings and said, "Whores."

"Oh, you want to try a whore?"

"I just . . . well, yeah . . . to get my mind off . . . yeah."

"Wait here."

Rawlings closed the door, then reopened it a few moments later and shoved Fancy out, only half dressed.

"She's all yours for the night," he said. "Don't hurt him, Fancy."

"But—but—I thought she was yours," Clooney said.

"Hey, she belongs to whoever pays for her."

"You paid for me," Fancy reminded him.

"But I'm giving you to him for the night," Rawlings said. "You treat him right, you hear?" He turned to Clooney and added, "I'll just get myself another one."

With that Rawlings went off down the hall and down the stairs to the lobby and, Clooney presumed, outside to find himself another whore.

Fancy, a full-bodied, dark-haired girl, grabbed his hand and said, "Come on, honey. Which room is yours?"

When he didn't answer right away, she said, "I won't hurt you. Honest. Which one's yours?"

"Two doors down," he said finally. "Number eleven."

"Well, let's go," she said, "we don't have all night—well, wait a minute. Yes, we do have all night."

And they did.

Now she was gone, after giving him a night to remember. She had done things with him that no other woman ever had, and he'd had his fair share of women. She had shown him things they could do with their mouths. . . .

But still, she wasn't Kate McElroy. She was just a whore, paid to do the things she did, and he couldn't stop thinking about Kate. Maybe if he went back to the Queen of Spades and talked to her. She'd be there by now, starting to deal. Or maybe he should wait awhile, give it some more time. He could go on over after dinner, sit at her table, take it easy, show her that he wasn't the type who got so upset they couldn't talk about it.

Maybe that was it. Maybe she was testing him, and in order to pass the test he had to come back.

There was a knock on the door then, and he knew it would be Rawlings. The door was still unlocked from when Fancy had left.

"Come in."

Rawlings came in, grinning from ear to ear.

"Well?"

"Well what?"

"How was she?"

"She was . . . amazing."

"I told you," Rawlings said, rubbing his hands together, "there's nothing like a whore."

"I guess not."

"So now this business with the blackjack dealer is over?"

Clooney didn't answer.

"Oh, come on, Dan."

"I can't help it, Mike."

"But didn't she make it clear—"

"I don't think so," Clooney said. "I don't think she made it clear at all. I—I just want to talk to her."

"Maybe we should just leave town, Dan," Rawlings suggested. "Maybe the idea of having a little R and R here was a bad idea. We've got things to do, you know. There are job—''

"I'm not ready for another job, Mike," Clooney said. "Not until I get this settled."

"And when will that be?"

"Today, maybe tomorrow . . . I don't know . . . I'm just askin' for some time. You owe me that, don't you?"

Rawlings stuck his little finger in his ear and dug a bit at an itch.

"Maybe I do," he said. "Hell, if Fancy couldn't turn you around, then maybe you do have to get things settled. Women . . . they can ruin a man, Dan. Just keep that in mind."

"I will, Mike," Clooney promised, "I will."

"I guess I can give you another few days," Rawlings said, "but just remember, our money's not gonna last forever, and we've got Beckett and Harper coming to meet us here. The next job is all set."

"I remember," Clooney said. "By the time they get here I'll be ready."

Rawlings shook his head again.

"Maybe we should have gone to Mexico with them," he said. "I hear those Mexican whores are wild. . . ."

TWENTY-FIVE

There were no mind games today. When Clint walked over to Kate McElroy's blackjack table she looked him straight in the eye.

"You're my first customer," she said.

"I thought I'd get to you before you got warmed up."

"Let's see if you did."

He bet five dollars and she dealt the first hand. She turned her hand over immediately, revealing blackjack. He had gotten twenty. A good hand, but not good enough.

"I guess you're warm," he said.

She gathered the cards up and said, "I'm always warm, Mr. . . ."

"Adams," he said, "Clint Adams."

"Oh, yes," she said, "you're the man who's quite famous."

"I detect an Eastern accent," he said.

"Philadelphia," she said. "Ever been there?"

"Once or twice. Nice city."

"Boring," she said. "Another hand?"

"Sure," he said, putting up another five dollars, "why not?"

That one he won, nineteen to eighteen.

"Well, we're even," he said.

"Would you like to quit even?"

"No self-respecting gambler wants to break even, Miss McElroy—or may I call you Kate?"

"Kate's fine," she said. "What shall I call you? Mr. Gunsmith?"

"No," he said, "Clint will do just fine."

"Where's your friend today, Clint?"

"Oh," he said, "I think maybe you wore him out."

"Did he tell you all about it?"

"A gentleman never tells."

"But who says he's a gentleman, right?" she asked. "He told you, all right, and now it's your turn?"

"Are you done with him?"

She smiled.

"I'm always done with a man before he's done with me, Clint."

Up close she was devastatingly beautiful, with lovely pale, smooth skin and a long graceful neck. She wore her hair up, and he found himself wondering what it would look like tumbling down over her pale, naked shoulders.

Clint believed everything Hartman had told him about Kate McElroy, but he also knew that Hartman didn't like the kind of woman Kate had turned out to be. Clint liked strong women, while his friend did not, so Kate McElroy was certainly more his type than Hartman's.

"I don't think Rick liked me, Clint," Kate said, gathering the cards up. "What do you think?"

"You're not his type."

"And what type is that?"

"Soft, passive," Clint said. "Rick likes to be in charge."

"Then you're right, I am definitely not his type," she said. "Am I yours?"

"Well," he said, leaving his ten-dollar bet, "I guess that remains to be seen."

She dealt him blackjack, and suddenly he had twenty-five dollars.

"So far," he said, "you are."

"The night is young," she said warningly.

"Deal the cards."

They played blackjack for hours, while other men came, played, lost, and moved on. After three hours they were pretty even.

"What do you say to raising the stakes?" he asked. "Or do you have to check with your boss?"

"I run my own table, Clint," she said. "Why don't you just bet whatever you think you can afford, and we'll take it from there?"

Clint put up fifty dollars and said, "Deal."

They started to draw a crowd when Clint started to win. When he did, Kate paid him in chips, so the chips began to pile up in front of him. He was having an incredible run of luck. At one point he bet one hundred dollars, won, let the two hundred ride, got blackjack, let the five hundred ride and won again, making an even thousand. People around the table began to wonder if he was going to bust Kate's table. Just as he started having visions of doing that, he started to lose, and that drew more of a crowd.

"Why doesn't he quit?" someone asked in a loud whisper that everyone could hear. "He's got an awful lot of her money."

"Shhh!" someone else said.

Clint knew he could quit now and be way ahead. He didn't know how far ahead he was because he hadn't been keeping count. He was afraid now that if he did count, he would quit, but he was enjoying the game too much to worry about the money. Of course, if he'd been losing his own money it might have been a different story, but the fact of the matter was he wasn't.

And so they played on.

TWENTY-SIX

At one point Rick Hartman had come into the saloon and seen the crowd around Kate's table. Instinctively, he knew what that meant. Kate and Clint had attracted each other's attention. He didn't have to worry about any awkward moments with Kate.

There was plenty of room at the bar because so many people were watching the game. He ordered a beer and Carla appeared at his elbow.

"You're his friend, aren't you?"

He looked at her. Clint had been right; she was a cute thing, and she did have a body that was built for bed. If she had ever applied for a job in his place he would have hired her in a minute.

"If you mean Clint, then the answer's yes."

"She's got him," Carla said sadly.

"Kate?"

"Yes."

"She's beating him?"

"No," Carla said, "the last I heard she was in danger of having her table broke."

"Oh."

"I mean she has him," Carla said. "She's got his attention. I know what will happen tonight."

"What's that?"

"He'll leave with her."

"Well," he said, "to get back at him, you could leave with me."

Carla looked at him with interest.

"You were with her last night, weren't you?"

"That's right."

"And you don't want to be with her tonight?"

"Right again."

"And you want me?"

"That's three in a row. You win."

"What do I win?"

"Come with me tonight," he said, "and find out."

Now she gave him her full attention, studying him boldly.

"All right," she said finally. "One o'clock."

He smiled and said, "I'll be here."

She nodded and went off to work the room. A man who had been watching the game made his way to the bar for a drink.

"How are they doing?" Hartman asked.

"He almost had her," the man said, waiting for his beer. "He almost had her closed down, but now she's coming back."

The man picked up his beer and took it back to the action.

"Not interested in watching?" the bartender asked.

Hartman shook his head.

"I know what happens when two people play cards for hours and hours."

"What?"

"They break even."

"Got your own place?"

"Yes."

"Thought so," the man said and went off to serve another customer.

Hartman took his beer to Kyle Merchant's private table and sat there to wait. He'd spent some time at some of the other gambling halls, played some blackjack and roulette here and there, and he was ahead a few hundred dollars. At one time he had been a true gambler, a man who did it for a living, but then he found out that it paid off to be the house, and that was when he started running his own places.

He looked around. Would he want to run a place of this size? He really hadn't made up his mind yet.

He looked over at the blackjack table and saw a man walking toward him. He recognized Ben Thompson.

"May I sit?" Thompson asked when he reached the table.

"Please."

"Guess we've heard about each other from the same source," Thompson said. "Clint Adams."

"I guess so."

Thompson looked over at the crowd.

"I guess he and Kate must be putting on a show."

"Looks like it."

"I thought poker was his game."

"It is, but he knows the rules of blackjack."

Thompson looked at Hartman.

"It pays to know the rules, no matter what you're doing."

Hartman met Thompson's gaze steadily.

"What does that mean exactly, Ben? Can I call you Ben?"

"Sure, Rick," Thompson said. "I'll tell you what it means. It means I think I know why you're here."

"Here in the Queen of Spades, or here in town?" Hartman asked.

"Just here," Thompson said. "It was Merchant, wasn't it? He and Crays want to replace me, and they've offered you the job. Am I right?"

"If somebody offered me a job," Hartman said, "I'm under no obligation to tell you."

Thompson glared at Hartman.

"If you've been offered my job, Mr. Hartman," he said coldly, "you'd better think twice about accepting, because it isn't available."

"I'll keep that in mind, Mr. Thompson."

They weren't on a first name basis anymore. Thompson stood up to leave.

It had been many years since Hartman had attracted the hostility of a man like Ben Thompson. He was starting to think that maybe he should never have left Labyrinth in the first place.

TWENTY-SEVEN

"Nineteen," Kate said, "pay twenty."

Clint turned his cards over, showing eighteen.

"You lose," Kate said, "again."

A groan went up from the crowd.

"Better quit," somebody said.

"His luck will change back," another voice said.

"Let me through," a third voice said, and Clint recognized it as that of Ben Thompson.

The crowd parted and Thompson appeared at Kate's left elbow.

"Game's over," he said.

"What's wrong, Ben?" Clint asked. "Nervous?"

"What do you mean, the game's over?" Kate demanded.

"You're taking too much attention away from the other tables," Thompson said.

97

"I run my own table, Ben," Kate said. "Anybody is welcome to sit in at any time."

"You've got yourself a private game going here, Kate," Ben said. "If that's the case, take it someplace else. I'm closing you down . . . now!"

Thompson looked across the table at Clint.

"You got a problem with that?"

"Not me, Ben," Clint said with a smile. "I'm ahead."

"That's it!" Thompson yelled. "Show's over. Either gamble at some other table, or get out!"

Kate glared at Thompson, then turned to Clint. She cashed in his chips for him, said, "Wait for me," and stomped off.

Clint collected his money and looked at Thompson, who was covering Kate's table.

"It's not very good policy to yell at your patrons, Ben."

"You better tell your friend to find himself a job somewhere else, Clint," Thompson said. "Trying for mine isn't going to be very healthy for him."

"Did he tell you he was after your job?"

"He didn't have to," Thompson said. "I knew that Merchant and Crays would want to replace me eventually. They're weasels."

"Don't you have a signed agreement?"

"Yes, I do."

"Then what's the problem?"

"No signature on a piece of paper ever stopped a bullet."

"You think they'd kill you to get rid of you?"

"I think they'd try."

Clint locked his eyes on Thompson's.

"But not themselves."

"Definitely not," Thompson said. "They're both too cowardly for that. They'll hire someone."

"Ben," Clint said, "you don't think that's why I'm here, do you?"

"The one thing I know about you, Clint," Thompson said, "is that you'd never hire out to kill someone. If you were going to come at me, it would be for your own reasons."

"And I don't have any, right now."

"I believe you," Thompson said, "but talk to your friend. It's for his own good."

"I'll keep it in mind, Ben."

"Good." Thompson looked at the money in front of Clint. "Congratulations on your good luck."

"Yeah, thanks."

Thompson went back to his office, and the crowd that had been around the table was evenly dispersed among the other tables.

Clint picked up his money and walked to the table where Hartman was sitting. Hartman had had the fore-sight to order two fresh beers. Carla had brought them over and brushed against his shoulder with her hip. She ignored Clint as they passed each other.

"What's wrong with her?" Clint asked.

"She was feeling ignored."

"Was?"

Hartman nodded.

"Not anymore."

Clint sat across from him and sipped from his beer.

"Are we switching girls tonight?"

"Looks like it."

"That might be interesting."

"Yes."

"But let's not do it again anytime soon."

"Right," Hartman agreed, and they toasted to it.

"What did Ben have to say?" Hartman asked.

"Just that I should warn you about trying to take his job."

"He warned me about that himself."

"Did he?"

Hartman nodded.

"While you were playing blackjack," he said. "You, uh, *were* playing blackjack over there, weren't you? I couldn't see much."

"Yes, I was playing blackjack."

"How'd you do?"

"I was hot for a while. Ben came along just when she was starting to get some of her money back."

"What have you got there?"

"A five-dollar chip," he said. "She missed it when she cashed me out."

"What are you going to do with it?"

"Play it on the roulette wheel."

"What number?"

"It doesn't matter," Clint said.

"What do you mean?"

"Whatever number I play will win."

"What?"

"You heard me."

"You're crazy."

"Think so?"

"Play it, then."

"Let's make it interesting."

Hartman sat back.

"What did you have in mind?"

"A wager."

"What kind of wager?"

"If my number hits," Clint said, "you have to make up your mind tonight about the job. If you say no, we leave tomorrow."

"And if your number doesn't hit?"

Clint shrugged.

"Whatever you say."

"Let me think."

By the time he was ready Clint had finished his beer.

"Okay," Hartman said, "if I win—that means if you lose . . . I mean, if your number doesn't come up—"

"Come on, get to it."

"I get another day to make up my mind."

"That's it?"

Hartman spread his hands.

"That's all."

"Let's go, then."

Clint and Hartman stood up and headed for the roulette wheel just as Kate came back out. She intercepted them on the way to the wheel.

"What's going on?"

"I've got one chip left and I'm playing it on the roulette wheel."

"What number?" she asked.

"He says it doesn't matter," Hartman said. "Whatever number he plays will come up."

She looked surprised and followed along.

When they got to the wheel it was already in motion,

so they waited for it to stop. It stopped on number twenty-four. There were three men at the table, and none of them had it.

"What number are you going to play?" Hartman asked.

Clint shrugged and said, "Might as well play twenty-four again."

"It just came up," one of the other men said.

"I know," Clint said, "that's why I can play it to come up *again*."

The three men laughed.

"A number don't hardly ever come up two times in a row," one of them said.

Clint put his five-dollar chip on number twenty-four and then stepped back to watch the wheel.

"Any other bets?"

The three men spread some chips around.

"Wait," Hartman said, "I want to buy some chips."

He tossed fifty dollars on the table and received ten five-dollar chips. He then stacked them on top of Clint's.

"All on the same number?" Kate asked.

"The man is amazingly lucky," Hartman said.

"Oh, I know that firsthand," she said.

"No more bets," the man said, and the wheel was going one way and the little white ball the other.

TWENTY-EIGHT

"Did you set that up?" Kate asked as they walked to her rooms.

"How would I do that?" he asked. "I don't know anyone who works at the saloon."

"But—but you hit twenty-four, and it had just come up," she said. "How did you do that?"

"I want to leave tomorrow."

"So?"

He told her about his bet with Hartman.

"How did you know you'd win?"

"I had nothing to lose by saying I'd win," Clint said. "The number came up, so I look good."

"And if it hadn't come up?"

"Then I would have lost, like everyone else does."

She shook her head as they stopped at her door, which was between the hardware store and an apothecary. She unlocked it and they went inside and up a flight of stairs.

"Your friend was here last night," she said.

"I know."

Inside, she turned to face him.

"That doesn't bother you?"

"No."

"Why not?"

"Because I'm not him."

He pulled her to him and kissed her. Her body felt slender, but taut and firm. She pressed her crotch tightly against him and wound her fingers in his hair as the kiss lengthened and deepened.

"Sit on the bed," she said.

"No."

He'd already been warned that she liked to be in charge, so he was determined not to let her.

"Come on," she said, "I want to undress for you."

"No," he said again, "I want to undress you."

He reached behind her and undid her dress before she could protest. He tugged it down her arms until it was gathered at her waist. Her breasts were bare beneath the dress, no undergarments to interfere with her flashing her cleavage at customers to distract them from their cards. Her breasts were smaller than Carla's, but they were firm, and the nipples were roughly the same size as the younger woman's. Of course, the smaller breasts made the nipples look even larger.

Clint got down on his knees and began to kiss her breasts, licking and sucking the nipples while he peeled the dress the rest of the way down. When it was around her ankles, she stepped out of it and kicked it away. She had on a slip and panties, and he quickly removed them,

as well. That done she was naked, and still wearing high
heels. Her legs were long and well toned, the high heels
showing them off beautifully.

He turned her around then, completely, once, then
twice.

"Do you like what you see?"

She had a body that did not have an ounce of fat on
it. He usually liked a little more meat on his women, but
she would do.

"You'll do."

She stepped back and put her hands on her hips.

"Is that so?"

He stood up.

"Why don't you get undressed now so we can see if
you'll do?" she said.

"All right."

He undressed in front of her, not the least bit uncom-
fortable beneath her gaze. He was comfortable with his
body. There wasn't an ounce of fat there, either, although it took no great effort on his part. He had always
been built that way, ever since he was a young man.

By the time he was naked he was also erect.

"Yes," she said, staring at his rigid penis. "Yes,
you'll do nicely."

She walked toward him and took one of his hands in
hers. She led him to the bed.

"Lie down," she said, "and I'll make you very
happy."

"No," he said.

"No?"

"That's what I said."

"But . . . you want me. I can see that."

"Yes, I want you," he said, "but I don't want you to service me. I want us to make each other happy."

"But . . . you'll see, you won't want to . . ."

"Lie on the bed with me, Kate."

"But I can't . . . I mean, I never . . ."

He kissed her then, holding her tightly, sliding his hands down so that he was cupping her butt.

"Come to bed," he said softly, "come to bed with me . . ."

By morning Kate was more exhausted than she had ever been. She had never before had any of the feelings she'd had that night with Clint. At one point he was nestled down between her legs, his lips and mouth and tongue working on her until suddenly she felt a burning sensation that started there and spread throughout her body. She actually thought she was going to die, and no man had *ever* made her feel that way before.

"Can you do that," she gasped, "all the time?"

"I can if you can," he'd said, smiling.

And they did, several times during the night. Now it was morning and she had to remind herself what her main goal was. She had to put the night behind her— for now—and move ahead with her plan.

"Clint?"

"Yes?"

"I have something to ask you."

Here it comes, he thought.

"Do you like money?"

"Very much."

"A lot of it?"

"I don't need a lot of it."

She propped herself up on her elbow and said, "Everybody needs a lot of it."

"Not me."

"How much do you need?"

"Oh," he said, "just enough, I guess."

"Enough for what?"

"To do what I want to do."

"And what's that?"

"I don't know," he said with a shrug. "It changes all the time."

"What if I told you I could fix it so you'd have enough money to do what you wanted to do, no matter what it was, and no matter when?"

"I guess I'd have to ask if it was legal."

"And if it wasn't?"

"Then I'd want no part of it."

"Really?"

"Really."

"You mean with your reputation—"

"There's nothing in my reputation that says I was ever dishonest."

"I see."

She lay down on her back.

"Was there something you wanted to ask me?"

"No," she said, "nothing. Will you be leaving today?"

"I won my bet last night, didn't I?"

"Yes," she said, "along with a lot of money."

"Then we'll be leaving today."

"When?"

"Just as soon as Rick gives Merchant and Crays his

decision about running the Queen of Spades.''

"And what's that decision going to be?''

"He'll be heading back to Labyrinth and his own place.''

"That's good,'' she said, "he won't have to deal with Ben Thompson, then.''

"No, he won't.''

She rolled over toward him and pressed herself against him.

"Before you go?''

"Yes?''

"Can we . . .'' She continued the question with her hands.

He laughed and said, "We can.''

TWENTY-NINE

"So?" Hartman asked.

"So what?"

"So what happened?"

They were having breakfast at the same café as the day before.

"A gentleman never tells, Rick."

"I told you."

"See what I mean?"

"Clint—"

"Okay, okay," Clint said. "She was . . . wonderful."

"Really? She didn't want to be in control?"

"Oh, she wanted to be," Clint said, "but forewarned *is* forearmed, you know."

"And what about, uh, finishing?"

"She did."

Hartman stared at him.

"Are you telling me the truth?"

"You asked me, didn't you? Why wouldn't I tell you the truth?"

"What did you do to her?"

Clint grinned and said, "Everything. She said we did everything that she had never done with a man before."

"That's amazing," Hartman said.

"Not so amazing."

"What do you mean?"

"Well, if I'd gone first and warned *you* about her, then you would have been able to do what I did."

"Well . . . yeah, that's right."

"See? So it wasn't so amazing."

"Uh . . . maybe not . . ." But Hartman didn't sound convinced. "What about the other thing?" he asked. "Did she ask you to help her rob the casino?"

"No . . . not in so many words."

"What do you mean?"

"Well, she asked me how I felt about money, and we talked about enough money and a lot of money and too much money and—"

"And she didn't ask you?"

"I told her I would never do anything illegal."

"So she didn't ask you."

"No."

"Do you think she's serious about it?"

"No."

"Why not?"

"I think if she was serious then she would have asked me."

"Maybe we should warn Thompson, though."

"I don't think Ben would believe us."

"Why not?"

"If the man who was trying to take your job came to you and told you something like that, would you believe him?"

"But I'm not after his job."

"Okay, if the man you *thought* was after your job told you that, would you believe him?"

"No."

"There."

"But he might believe you."

"I don't think so."

"What about the sheriff?"

"What about him?"

"We could tell him."

"Rick," Clint said, "why don't we just do what we were going to do and leave?"

"I have to find Merchant and give him my decision."

"Okay, then, let's do that and head back to Labyrinth."

"Can I finish my breakfast first?"

"Go ahead."

"You're buying, right?"

"What?"

"You won big last night."

"Who put fifty dollars down on my number at the last minute?" Clint asked. "You're not exactly in the poorhouse either."

Hartman shook his head and laughed.

"On one turn of the wheel," he said. "It was worth losing the bet."

THIRTY

After Clint left her room, Kate McElroy remained in her bed, thinking. If she'd been looking for a man to make her happy, Clint Adams would have been that man. Unfortunately, she was looking for a man for another reason, and while he or Rick Hartman would have been smart enough, neither of them was willing.

She wondered how hard it would be to get back into the good graces of Dan Clooney.

Clint and Hartman found Kyle Merchant and Robert Crays in their office.

"Good morning," Merchant said as they entered. "Have you come to tell us your decision?"

"I think we're going to be moving on, Kyle," Hartman said. "I appreciate the offer, but I don't think I'll be taking the job."

"It's probably just as well," Merchant said.

"Why is that?" Clint asked.

"Kyle spent last night with our lawyer, and he can't find any way for us to get out of our agreement with Ben Thompson."

"That's right," Merchant said, "unless the saloon gets robbed, Thompson's job is safe."

"That's in the contract?" Clint asked.

"Yes," Crays said.

"If that happened how would it be his fault and cost him his job?"

"The security of the place is his responsibility," Merchant said. "If he fails in that, he's out."

"Sorry, Rick," Crays said.

"Hey, forget it," Hartman said. "You'd owe me an apology if I'd said yes."

"Well, I'm sorry we put you in this position, anyway."

All four men shook hands, wished each other luck, and then Clint and Hartman left.

"Did you hear that?" Hartman asked. "Their loophole clause with Ben?"

"I heard it."

"What do you think of Kate's idea now?"

"All the more reason to believe she's not serious," Clint said. "Ben's security has to be tight, and she'd know that. Come on, let's just head back to Labyrinth, where it's quiet. You know, I actually thought I'd like a town that was all about gambling."

"So did I," Hartman said. "I guess there is such a thing as too much of a good thing."

• • •

Kate was standing at her window when Clint Adams and Rick Hartman went by on their horses, on their way out of town. It took all of her willpower not to run after Clint. He'd made her feel the way no other man ever had—the way she never thought any man could. At another time in her life she would have tried to make him stay, even just a little longer. If he stayed now, however, he'd just get in her way. She watched until she couldn't see them any longer, then moved away from the window. She needed a bath, then she'd get dressed and see if she could find Dan Clooney.

"So what do we do now?" Crays asked Merchant after Clint and Hartman left.

"We explore other options," Merchant said.

"What other options?"

Merchant smiled.

"I don't know," he said, "I guess we'll just have to think of some."

THIRTY-ONE

It was a full day later when they heard the news. They were in a town called Rockland, still in Nevada. They had stopped only for a few supplies, and to get a drink. Their horses were tied up outside the saloon, and they were at the bar.

Suddenly, a man came running in and looked around wildly. He looked like someone who had news to tell and was looking for someone to tell it to. Clint and Hartman didn't want to be those men, so they turned back to the bar.

The bartender, however, was not as smart.

"What the hell do ya want, Willie?" he yelled.

"It just come over the wire," the man said.

"What did?"

"The news."

"What news?"

Now the man looked around again, wiping at his mouth with one hand. Clint could see him in the mirror. Obviously, he was looking to trade the news for a drink. That was the reason he was looking around so wild-eyed.

"Give him a drink," Clint said. "I'll pay."

The bartender scowled but poured a shot glass of whiskey.

"Thanks, mister," Willie said and tossed the drink back.

"Now what's your news, Willie?" the bartender asked.

"It's about that new town, Queensville?"

"What about it?" the barman asked, becoming impatient.

"It's been robbed."

"What?" Hartman said, turning around quickly.

"Yes," Willie said, wiping his mouth, "robbed."

"Give him another drink," Hartman said. "I'm buying this time."

The barman poured it.

"Thanks, mister," Willie said and did away with it.

"No more drinks until you tell all your news, Willie," Clint said.

"Well, that's it," Willie said. "They got robbed."

"The whole town?" the bartender asked.

"Well, no, not the whole town," Willie said. "How can you rob a whole town?"

"Then who got robbed?" Hartman asked.

"The big place," Willie said, "what's it called?"

"The Queen of Spades?"

"That's the one!"

"When was it hit?" Clint asked.

"Early this morning," Willie said, "leastways, that's when they found out."

"And how did you find out?" the bartender asked.

"It come in over the wire, for the sheriff."

And Willie had been waiting outside the telegraph office, waiting for some piece of news to come in that would be worth a drink to somebody.

"We've got to go—" Hartman started, but Clint grabbed his arm to stop him.

"Let's take our beer to a table."

"But—"

"We've got to talk, Rick."

"About what?"

"Bring your beer."

Hartman picked up his beer and walked to a table.

"Give him one more drink," Clint said, tossing a coin on the bar and then following Hartman.

"You heard what he said," Hartman said as Clint sat down. "She went ahead with it. We should go tell the sheriff."

"We don't have any proof it was her," Clint said.

"Well, we can tell him we think it was her."

"And if it wasn't we'd be putting her in a lot of trouble."

"So what do we do?"

Clint rubbed his jaw.

"I guess one of us should have taken her more seriously," Clint said, "instead of just dealing with the issue of sex."

"And that means . . . ?"

"I think we'd better head back," Clint said. "It might

be better for her if we find her before anyone else does."

"You're not worried about the sheriff there, are you?" Hartman asked.

"No," Clint said, "but Ben Thompson is not going to take this lightly, and I don't think Crays and Merchant will either."

"But what can we do?" Hartman asked. "We don't know which way she went."

"We'll find out all we need to know when we get there, Rick," Clint said, "and if we leave now we can be there before dark tomorrow."

Hartman shook his head.

"I thought we left that town behind us for good."

"One more visit," Clint said. "Hopefully, that will be it."

They finished their beers and stood up. Willie was still standing by the bar, staring at his empty glass.

"You're not gettin' any more, Willie," the bartender said, "so get moving."

"I got one more piece of information," Willie said, looking at Clint and Hartman.

"And what's that?" Clint asked.

"He's lyin'," the bartender said.

"Willie?" Clint said.

"I ain't lyin', mister," Willie said, "honest."

Clint took out a coin and put it in the man's shirt pocket. He was surprised that up close Willie looked thirty, and before he'd estimated the man's age at around fifty.

"You can buy your own drink," Clint said. "What's the rest of it?"

"The telegram to the sheriff said that the robbers might be headed this way."

Clint and Hartman exchanged a glance.

"Well," Clint said, "I guess we better talk to the sheriff here after all."

THIRTY-TWO

The sheriff's name was Jess Thornton, and for once Clint hoped that the man would react to his name.

"I know who you are, Mr. Adams," Thornton said. He was in his thirties, a competent-looking man with intelligent eyes. "What brings you to Rockland?"

"We're actually just passing through, Sheriff," Clint said, "on our way back to Texas from Queensville."

"Queensville," the sheriff said, looking surprised. "Did you hear what happened there? When were you there?"

"We left yesterday, and yes, we heard something today, but not the whole story. We have some friends there, and we're hoping no one was hurt. I wonder if you could fill us in."

"Well, I can tell you that somebody definitely was hurt. One man was killed."

120

"And who was that?"

"A fella named Crays, Robert Crays. I understand he founded the town with a partner."

"Crays is dead?" Hartman asked.

"That's what I was told," Thornton said. "I received a telegram from Ben Thompson."

"Why would Ben Thompson send you a telegram?" Clint asked. "I mean, I know he's the manager of the Queen of Spades, but—"

"He's apparently got himself a new job," Thornton said.

"And what would that be?" Clint asked.

"He's the new sheriff in Queensville."

"Sheriff?" Clint asked. "What happened to the old sheriff? When did Ben get the job?"

"I don't know the answers to those questions, Mr. Adams," Thornton said. "I only know that Sheriff Ben Thompson says that the robbers left town going in this direction. Now, unless they double back, they're headed this way, and I've got to get a posse together, which has never been an easy task in this town."

Clint and Hartman looked at each other, because they both knew what the sheriff was thinking even before the man knew it himself.

"Hey, wait a minute," Thornton said. "You fellas said you had friends in Queensville. Was this fella Crays one of them?"

"We knew him, yeah," Clint said.

"Well, then, you boys will want to be on the posse, won't you?"

"Will we?" Hartman asked Clint.

Clint scowled and said, "I guess so."

"Good, I'll swear you in—"

"Why don't you just consider us sworn in, Sheriff," Clint suggested. "Don't even bother with badges."

"I don't have extra badges, anyway," Thornton said. "I don't know how many more men I'm gonna be able to get, but why don't we meet out front here in an hour."

"Sure," Clint said, "why not?"

"We'll be there."

When Clint and Hartman left the sheriff's office, they went back to the only familiar place in town, the saloon. The same bartender was still there, and there were a couple of other men at the bar, but Willie was gone.

"Now we're on a posse," Hartman said, shaking his head as they sat down with two more beers.

"Look, if Kate is headed this way and we're going to help her, that's where we have to be."

"Why should we help her?" Hartman asked. "I mean, if she robbed the casino and killed a man—"

"We don't know that she did."

"Okay," Hartman said, "so if she didn't, what are we doing on a posse?"

Clint stared at his friend for a few moments, then said, "That's a good question."

He stood up.

"Where are we going now?"

"Why don't you just wait here," Clint suggested. "I'm going to go find the telegraph office."

"What for?"

"To find out for sure if Kate was involved or not."

"You going to send a telegram to Ben Thompson?"

"Mmm, I don't think so. Besides, if he's the sheriff he's probably out of town leading a posse of his own."

"Who, then?"

"Merchant, I guess," Clint said. "He appears to be the only one left."

"Okay," Hartman said, "I might as well wait here. It doesn't take two men to send a telegram."

"I'll be back as soon as I can," Clint said.

"You better get back before the posse leaves," Hartman said. "If I have to go, so do you."

"I'll be back."

Clint was back in forty minutes.

"I waited for the answer."

"How did you word your question?"

"I asked for detailed information on the robbery, because I wanted to help. Merchant responded."

"And?"

"He says they're not sure who pulled the robbery, but they think it was four men."

"No woman?"

"Well . . . according to Merchant, Kate McElroy was taken, as well."

"What?"

"That's what he said."

"But . . . what if that was her plan?" Hartman asked. "To make it look like she was kidnapped."

"That could be."

"I wonder where she got four men on such short notice," Hartman said.

"Maybe the notice wasn't so short."

"What do you mean?"

"Remember the fella who wanted to fight you for her?" Clint asked.

"Vaguely."

"He had a friend in town," Clint said. "His name was Rawlings."

"Don't know him."

"If she got those two, and then they got two more . . ."

"You think that fella would help her after the way she treated him?"

"For a chance at Kate *and* money?" Clint asked. "What do you think?"

Hartman checked the time and said, "I think we've got a posse to join."

As Clint and Hartman approached the sheriff's office, leading their horses behind them, they didn't see anyone there. There was one horse tied to a hitching post, which they assumed was the sheriff's.

"What the hell—" Hartman said.

"The sheriff did warn us that he usually has trouble putting a posse together."

Just then the door to the office opened and Sheriff Thornton came walking out.

"What's going on, Sheriff?" Hartman asked.

"I'm real glad you boys made it."

"Where's everyone else?" Clint asked.

"I'm, uh, afraid there isn't anyone else," Thornton said. "I have enough trouble putting a posse together when there's trouble here in town. Nobody was really concerned with Queensville's problem."

"So it's just the three of us?" Clint asked.

"That's right—that is, if you fellas are still volunteering. If not, I guess I'll be going alone."

Clint looked at Hartman, who nodded.

"No, we're with you, Sheriff."

"Okay, then mount up," Thornton said, "and let's get moving."

THIRTY-THREE

Sam Beckett wondered how come with a woman along he got stuck with the cooking.

"It ain't right," he said to Brian Harper. "She should be cooking."

"Why don't you tell that to Clooney?" Harper asked.

They both looked over to where Dan Clooney and Mike Rawlings were sitting. Away from them, sitting by herself, was the woman, Kate McElroy.

"I would, if you'd back me up," Beckett said.

"Why should I?" Harper asked. "Nobody's askin' me to cook."

"That's because you're so bad at it."

"Yeah," Harper said, "I'm bad when I wanna be."

"You mean—don't tell me you can cook," Beckett said accusingly.

"Better than you."

"How come you never told nobody?"

"So I wouldn't get stuck doin' what you're doin' right now."

Beckett, a short, thickly built man in his thirties, stared at Harper, who was taller and thinner but also in his thirties. Harper had been riding with Clooney and Rawlings for a couple of years, while Beckett had come aboard only a few months before.

"It's because I'm the new guy, right?" Beckett asked. "That's it, ain't it?"

"No," Harper said.

"Then what?"

"It's because the woman is Clooney's woman, that's why."

Beckett looked over at the woman, then gave Harper a sly look.

"I may be the new guy," he said, "and maybe I ain't as smart as most, but I'm smart enough to know that woman don't belong to nobody."

Harper looked over at Kate, then nodded and said, "I think you're right."

The two men had arrived in Queensville and within an hour Clooney was telling them that they were going to rob the Queen of Spades saloon.

"How we gonna do that?" Harper had asked. "We got to plan—"

"We've got somebody on the inside," Clooney had said, "don't worry. All the plans are made. Just do as you're told."

Now they were on the run with a ton of money and a dead man behind them.

"You know," Beckett said to Harper, "with all the

jobs we pulled in the past few months nobody ever got killed. That was because of the planning.''

"So?"

"So this time a man got killed, and I still don't know how, or who killed him.''

"Why do you have to know?" Harper asked. "It's done, and we've got a lot of money to split.''

"That's another thing," Beckett said. "What's the split?''

"Don't worry," Harper said, "Clooney will let us know.''

"Sure," Beckett said under his breath, "after the woman lets him know.''

Harper heard him but pretended not to.

Dan Clooney walked over to the fire and asked Sam Beckett, "Is dinner ready yet?''

"It's ready.''

"Give me a plate for Kate.''

Beckett dished out beans and bacon wordlessly and handed it to Clooney. He then poured him a cup of coffee and handed him that, too.

"The rest of you can eat now.''

As Clooney walked over to Kate, Mike Rawlings came over to the fire.

"I think he's crazy," Beckett said while handing a plate to Rawlings, and then looked shocked, as if he just realized that he'd spoken out loud.

"You might be right," Rawlings said. "I guess we'll just have to see.'' Then Rawlings looked at Beckett and added, "In the future, though, keep your thoughts to yourself, okay?''

"Sure, Mike," Beckett said, "sure."

"Mike, when are things gonna get back to normal?" Harper asked.

"By normal you mean banks?"

Harper nodded.

"I don't know."

"We coulda took that bank in Queensville, you know?"

"With a little planning, yeah," Rawlings agreed, "we probably could of."

"Maybe," Harper said, "we still could."

Rawlings didn't respond to the statement at first, but then he turned his head and looked at Harper with interest.

Clooney carried the plate of food over to Kate McElroy, who accepted it.

"What are you thinking about?" Clooney asked. "The dead man? Crays?"

She had been thinking about Clint Adams, but she decided not to tell him that.

"Yes," she said, "Crays. Nobody was supposed to die, Dan. I had it planned out so that nobody would die."

"None of my people killed him, Kate," Clooney said. "I swear to you."

"Then who did?"

Clooney shrugged.

"I don't know, and to tell you the truth, I don't care. All I care about now is spending the money."

"They'll be after us, you know," she said. "Because of the murder, they'll be after us and they won't stop.

If it was only the money they probably would give up after a while, but not now.''

"So? Who'll come after us, that sheriff? He's nothing to worry about.''

"Thompson.''

"What?''

She looked at him.

"Ben will come. He won't take this lying down. The money from the casino was his responsibility.''

"You knew that all along.''

"I had hoped that he would cooperate.''

Clooney frowned.

"Did you sleep with him, too?'' he asked. "To get him to go along?''

She had told him that she slept with Clint Adams and Rick Hartman to try to recruit them.

"It didn't work with Adams and the other one, what made you think it would work with Thompson?''

"It used to work on any man,'' she said. "Maybe I'm just losing my touch.''

"Well, you ain't lost your touch with me,'' Clooney said. He took her arm. "I'll do anything for you, Kate, as long as you play straight with me. Understand?''

"I understand, Dan,'' she said. "Now will you let go of my arm?''

He matched stares with her for a few moments, then released her arm.

"You better go and get something to eat for yourself,'' she said, "and then get some sleep. We'll want to get an early start tomorrow.''

"All right.''

"We should cut the money up tomorrow,'' she said,

"so they can go their way and we can go ours."

He stopped in mid-step.

"What?"

"Well," she said, "we don't want them around us all the time, do we?"

"Well . . . no . . ."

"Once we give them their cut we can split up." She paused a moment, then said, "Unless . . ."

"Unless what?"

She looked down at the saddlebags that contained the money they had stolen from the casino.

"There's a lot of money in here, Dan," she said, "but when you start to cut it up, it's not so much. . . ."

He turned to face her.

"What are you saying?"

She stared at the saddlebags, then looked up at him and said, "Oh, nothing. I'm just thinking out loud is all. Go ahead, get something to eat."

As Clooney walked away she put her hand on the saddlebags, which bulged slightly, and rubbed.

THIRTY-FOUR

Ben Thompson looked around camp at his posse. Less than a day in the saddle and they were all moaning and complaining. To tell the truth his own butt was kind of sore, from all that time sitting in a leather chair.

He finished the beans he was eating and set the tin plate aside, then reached for his coffee. If it wasn't for the fact that Robert Crays had been found sitting in his chair, dead, he might not even be out here. Yes, the casino was his responsibility, but with the loophole in his agreement—which he hadn't known about, but now did—his job was gone already. Now he had a new job, as sheriff of Queensville. Merchant, who had only hours earlier informed him that he was out of a job as far as the Queen of Spades was concerned, had come to him and asked him to wear the badge.

"So you can fire me from this job, too?" he had asked.

''Ben,'' Merchant said, ''you're the only man in town who can find them. They robbed the casino and killed my partner. I personally guarantee you won't lose this job.''

''I don't want the job,'' Thompson said, ''but I'll take it because they killed Crays in my place—but I want it in writing. I have the sheriff's job until I choose to give it up.''

''I'll write it up,'' Merchant said.

''No loopholes.''

''No loopholes,'' Merchant promised.

So here he was, on the trail of four men and a woman who had robbed the casino and killed a man, costing him a cushy job. The other thing that rankled him was that Kate McElroy was part of it. Sure, it was possible that she'd been kidnapped, but he figured that the job had to have been planned from the inside, and as far as he was concerned, she was the most likely suspect.

Reading sign had never been a strong point of Thompson's. He was a gambler and, since the death of Wild Bill Hickok, handled a gun better than anyone he knew—in his opinion even better than Clint Adams. But tracking . . . that was something different, and he didn't have a decent tracker in his posse, just a bunch of merchants and gamblers he or Merchant had bullied into coming along. Nine men, none of whom could ride or shoot worth a damn. If only Clint Adams hadn't left town. They weren't friends, but Adams would have ridden with him, and he would have been able to count on him.

This group was ready to turn back, and if that happened he'd just have to go on alone. He'd keep heading east, and maybe he'd run into the posse from Rockland. Maybe they'd have a decent tracker with them.

"Mr. Thompson?"

He looked up at one of the men from the posse. He didn't know anyone's name, and didn't care to.

"What is it?"

"We've been talkin', sir, and—"

"Who's we?"

"Uh, the men, sir . . ."

"How many?"

"Uh, all of us."

"And?"

"We, uh, think we're going to turn back, sir. We're just not cut out for this kind of thing."

"Then turn back," Thompson said.

"We'll leave in the morning—"

"Now!"

"What?" The man frowned.

"If you're going to leave, leave now."

"But, sir, it's dark—"

"Any man who is still here in the morning," Thompson said, "is here for the duration."

"Uh, but—"

"And I'll shoot any man who tries to leave then. Do you understand?"

"Uh . . . yes, sir."

Thompson looked away, dismissing the man.

In a flurry of activity, over the next twenty minutes, they all collected their gear, saddled their horses, and started back to Queensville in the dark. Damned fools! Half of them would break their necks or lose their horses to broken legs before they got there.

After they were gone Thompson actually relaxed. He had always been more comfortable alone, and this was no exception. It had been a long time since he'd slept under the stars, and he found himself actually enjoying the solitude. Maybe when this was all over he'd get back in the saddle for a while, even if it was just to have some time to decide what to do with the rest of his life.

But that was after he brought these killers back to Queensville, so they could hang.

Thompson wondered, if Kate McElroy proved to be one of the robbers after all, if she'd be hung, also.

He couldn't remember the last woman he'd heard of being hung.

THIRTY-FIVE

Clint, Hartman, and Sheriff Jess Thornton had ridden a full day without seeing any sign of anyone. They camped for the night, set watches, and got an early start in the morning. They hadn't ridden an hour when they saw a lone rider approaching them.

"One man," Thornton said. "Know him?"

"Can't see him clearly yet," Clint said.

"Maybe the robbers split up already."

"Could be," Clint said, "but I wouldn't think so. Not yet."

"Why not?"

"They'd wait until they had gotten further away before they stopped to divide the money."

"Why?"

"Because along with dividing the spoils," Clint said, "goes arguments, and that takes a while."

"Clint?" Hartman said.

"What?"

"I think that's Ben."

Clint turned away from Thornton to look at the rider again. He saw the glint of the sun off of something shiny.

"Might be," Clint said. "He's wearing a badge. It's reflecting the sun."

They continued riding and after a few hundred yards Clint said, "That's Ben all right."

"But if that's Sheriff Thompson," Thornton said, "then the robbers aren't between us."

"No," Clint said, "they either headed north at some point or south."

"Can you track them, Mr. Adams?" Thornton asked.

"I'm not a good tracker."

"Neither am I," Hartman said.

"Neither is Ben," Clint said. "That leaves me, and yes, if we can find some sign, I can track them."

"Shall we wait here for Sheriff Thompson to reach us?" Thornton asked.

"No," Clint said, "we're going to have to go back the way he came, anyway, to look for sign. Let's just keep going until we meet up."

When they reached Ben Thompson they all reined in and faced each other.

"Sheriff Thompson?" Thornton said. "I'm Sheriff Thornton, of Rockland."

"Sheriff," Thompson said. "Hello, Clint, Hartman."

"Ben," Clint said.

"Looks like things got into a big mess back in

Queensville,'' Thompson said. ''The job might be waiting for you, Hartman.''

''Don't want it, Ben,'' Hartman said. ''Never did.''

Thompson looked at Thornton.

''I suppose they haven't come this far?''

''They didn't cross our path.''

Thompson sat up straight in his saddle and stretched.

''I guess they must have cut north or south at some point,'' he said.

''That's what we figured,'' Thornton said.

Thompson hesitated for a few moments, then looked at Clint.

''I can't track them, Clint.''

''I can, Ben,'' Clint said. ''Let's double back and see if we can pick up some sign.''

''Thanks,'' Thompson said, ''thanks a lot.'' He looked at Sheriff Thornton.

''I'll come along, too,'' Thornton said. ''I've come this far.''

''Much obliged for the help, Sheriff.''

Thompson turned his horse and fell in next to Clint.

''How'd you end up with that badge?'' Clint asked.

''Well, it seems I didn't read all the print when I signed my agreement to manage the Queen of Spades.'' He explained how Merchant had come to him with the offer of the badge, and why he'd taken it.

''Makes as much sense as anything, I guess,'' Clint said. ''You plan on staying on after this is through?''

''Naw,'' Thompson said. ''Once I bring back Crays's killer, and as much of the money as I can, I expect I'll be moving on.''

''Let me ask you something.''

Thompson looked at him.

"You want to know about your friend Kate?"

"Well, she's not exactly my friend," Clint said, "but yeah, that's what I was going to ask."

"Well, I have no proof," Thompson said, "but if I had to bet, I'd put my money on her planning the whole thing."

Clint and Hartman exchanged a glance in that moment, and they decided not to mention the fact that Kate had apparently not only planned the job, but had tried to recruit them, as well.

"What do you intend to do with her when you catch her?" Hartman asked.

"Damned if I know," Thompson said. "Do they hang women?"

"Sheriff Thornton?" Clint said.

Thornton shook his head and said, "Damned if I know that either."

"Well," Thompson said, "it'd be a shame to hang a woman looks like that."

"Ben?" Clint said.

"Yeah?"

"What happened to Crays? I mean, exactly."

"Don't know for sure," Thompson said. "All I know is he was sitting in my leather chair with a bullet in his chest when we found him."

"Was that before or after the place had been robbed?"

"Wasn't until after that we discovered the money was gone," Thompson said.

"And you figure it was four men?"

"Witnesses saw four men and a woman—most likely

Kate—riding away from the saloon early that morning."

"If they got into the place early and cleaned it out," Clint wondered, "why'd they need four men?"

"Lookouts, I guess," Thompson said, "and somebody to put a slug into Crays."

"Now there's another thing," Clint said. "What was Crays doing there?"

"Don't know."

"Could it be he was in on it, and they killed him rather than split it with him?"

"You know," Thompson said, "if one of those boys was going to rob his own place I'd bet on Merchant."

"Why?"

"He's just old enough and ornery enough to want to make off with it, but make it look like somebody else did. Crays, he's young enough to have done it and taken off, to start over somewhere else."

"You might have a point there," Clint said.

THIRTY-SIX

They backtracked several hours before they came to some sign.

"How do you know it's them?" Thornton asked.

Clint was on one knee, studying the tracks on the ground.

"I don't," Clint said, "but I can see that there are five distinctly different sets of tracks."

"There were four men and a woman, right?" the sheriff of Rockland asked.

"That's right," Clint said.

"Then they haven't split up."

"No," Clint said, "not at this point. What they've done here is head south."

"California?" Thornton asked.

"From here," Clint said, "it's more likely they're going to Arizona, and then on to Mexico."

Thornton looked at all three men and then settled on Thompson.

"We can't follow them to Arizona," he said, "and certainly not to Mexico."

"Why not?" Thompson asked.

"We have no jurisdiction."

"That doesn't matter," Thompson said.

"You could lose your job."

Thompson laughed.

"That doesn't matter either."

"It matters to me," Thornton said. "I'm sorry, I'd like to help, but I can't leave Rockland for that long."

"Then go back," Thompson said.

"I . . . I can go as far as Arizona with you—"

"That's not necessary," Thompson said. "You go on back, Sheriff. You've done your part."

Thornton looked at Clint and Hartman, and then back at Thompson.

"And do me a favor," Thompson said.

"What?"

Thompson unpinned his badge and tossed it to Thornton, who caught it awkwardly.

"Send that back to Queensville by messenger, will you?"

"You don't want it anymore?" Thornton asked, confused.

"I never did," Thompson said.

He ignored Thornton then and looked at Clint and Hartman.

"What about you fellas?"

"I'll stick with you awhile, Ben," Clint said.

"So will I," Hartman said.

"Okay, then," Thompson said, "we better get moving. How far ahead of us are they, Clint?"

"I won't be able to guess about that until we find one of their old campsites—and if they kept cold camp I might not even be able to guess."

"Doesn't matter, anyway," Thompson said. "I don't have a job anymore, so I guess I'll just make catching up to them my job."

"If you don't mind," Hartman said, "I do have a job, sort of, so I'll just make catching up to them a hobby."

"Whatever you call it," Thompson said, "I appreciate the help."

They finally did find an old campsite, and Clint pressed his hand down on the ashes of the fire.

"It's cooled," he said. "They're a full day ahead of us, maybe more."

"They're not moving very fast, then," Hartman said. "They should be further along."

"It's my guess," Clint said, "that Kate is slowing them down. I don't think she's spent much time in the saddle, Rick, do you?"

They were both thinking about what her nude behind had looked like.

"No," Hartman said, "I don't think so either."

"So maybe she was the brains behind the robbery," Thompson said, "but she's going to be the reason we catch up to them."

Clint mounted up.

"We should discuss what we're going to do if they split up," he said.

"If that happens then we'll split up," Thompson said.

"How?"

"I think that'll be your call, Clint," Thompson said. "You're the one reading the sign."

"Well," Clint said, "it looks like the same horse is in the lead, and one of the horses looks smaller than the rest. That's probably Kate's. I guess it will depend on who you want to catch up with the most."

"The money," Thompson said, "and my guess is that most of the money will be with Kate. My thinking is she got Dan Clooney and his friend, and probably another couple of their friends, to help her. Clooney was sniffing around her for days until you fellas came along."

Clint and Hartman exchanged a glance. They were waiting to see if Thompson was going to ask them if she'd tried to recruit them, but the question never came.

"I guess I'll make up my mind when the time comes," Clint said. "Maybe they'll stay together all the way to Mexico."

"That," Ben Thompson said, "would be the best news I've had in weeks."

THIRTY-SEVEN

The first night they camped in Arizona things finally came to a head.

"She's leading him around by his dick," Sam Beckett complained to Brian Harper.

"Maybe you just wish she was leading you around by your dick," Harper said.

"Come on, Brian," Beckett said, "I just want my money. When are they gonna split it up?"

Clooney had resisted Kate's suggestion of splitting the money up, and then splitting the gang up.

"We're safer together until we get where we're going," he told her. "We still don't know if there's a posse after us, and if there is, we don't know how many men there'll be."

"But I think splitting up would be safer," she said.

"Well, I don't," he replied. "Look, Kate, maybe you

planned the job, but I'm more experienced at this part.''

''Running?''

''Yes, running.''

''Well,'' she said, ''if we're going to stay together, then I'm going to hold on to the money. I don't think it should be split up until *we* split up.''

''That's fine,'' he said. ''Suit yourself.''

Now Beckett was getting real impatient, and Harper had to admit, he would have liked to have his share in his pocket.

''You're thinkin' the same thing, ain't ya?'' Beckett asked.

''Maybe I am,'' Harper said, ''but you heard Rawlings. Keep your thoughts to yourself.''

''You know what?''

''What?''

''I don't think Mike is too happy with the way things are either.''

''Maybe he ain't.'' Harper said. ''Why don't you go ask him?''

''You know,'' Beckett said, ''I think if we both asked him he'd give us an answer.''

''Rawlings and Clooney have been riding together a long time,'' Harper said. ''I don't think Mike will go against Dan.''

''We don't want him to go against Clooney,'' Beckett said, ''we just want what's ours. Jesus, from the minute we rode into Queensville we been on the go. I need some time to sit and think, ya know? With my share of the money, I could do that. Huh?''

They were sitting by the fire because Beckett was cooking again. Clooney was eating with Kate, while

Rawlings was off by himself eating alone.

"Come on, Brian," Beckett said. "Whataya say?"

Harper looked up and saw Rawlings approaching.

"Quiet."

But Rawlings knew something was up. He squatted to pour himself some more coffee and looked at both men.

"Okay," he said, setting the pot back down, "tell me what's going on."

"Whataya mean, Mike—"

"Don't lie to me, Brian," Rawlings said, cutting him off. "You two are up to something."

Harper and Beckett exchanged glances.

"Beckett's been complainin'—" Harper finally said.

"Not complainin'," Beckett said quickly. "I've just been, ya know, sayin' . . ."

"Saying what?" Rawlings asked.

Beckett looked to Harper for help, but Harper found something else to look at.

"Okay," he finally said, "Mike, I think she's trouble. Is she gonna stay with us from now on?"

Rawlings looked over his shoulder at Clooney and Kate, then back at Beckett.

"I don't know."

"Ain't you talked to him about it?"

"No."

"What about splitting the money up?" Harper asked, finally deciding to get involved. "When do we do that?"

"I don't know."

"Mike," Beckett said, "this ain't the way we been doing things, ya know?"

"I know," Rawlings said.

"So . . ." Beckett said.

"So what?"

"So somebody should talk to Clooney."

"You want to do it?" Rawlings asked.

"N-no," Beckett said, "I don't wanna do it. We thought . . . I thought . . . well, you and him are friends."

"Oh, you want me to do it."

"Well . . . yeah."

Rawlings looked at both of them, and then surprised them.

"Okay," Rawlings said, "I'll do it."

The other two men exchanged surprised looks.

"But you two have to back me up."

"What?" Beckett said.

"You heard me," Rawlings said. "I'll do the talkin', but you fellas have to back up whatever I say."

"Well," Beckett said, licking his lips, "w-what are you gonna say?"

"I don't know yet."

"And when?" Harper asked.

"I don't know that yet, either, but whenever it is, that's the way it's got to be. Okay?"

"Well . . . o-okay," Beckett said.

"Count me in," Harper said.

"All right."

"Look at them," Kate said.

"Who?" Clooney asked.

"Your friends," she said impatiently. "Look at them. They're plotting."

"They're not," he said.

"They want to take it all, Dan."

"That's not the way we do things, Kate."

"Well, I'm not usually around, am I?"

"No."

"Then this is not a usual situation."

"They wouldn't go against me."

"Why not?"

"They respect me."

"You mean they're afraid of you?"

"Oh," he said proudly, "you noticed, huh?"

What she had noticed was that Clooney was the leader, but she felt that was only the case because there was an acute lack of leadership ability in the other three men. Clooney was not a strong leader, but at least he took the initiative. Still, if the other three decided to go against them, she didn't know if Clooney could hold them off.

In the saddlebags with the money Kate had an old Navy Colt she had bought just before moving to Queensville. It was a big gun and she needed both hands to hold it steady, but she could hit what she fired at.

As for Clooney, she didn't exactly trust him either. That was the reason she still hadn't told him just how much money was in the saddlebags. She was afraid that his lust for the money might outweigh his lust for her.

After all, she was not as young as she used to be, which was the reason she had planned this job in the first place.

She didn't want to argue with Clooney on the question of a posse. She didn't think there was one, but she did think that Ben Thompson would be on their trail. His ego would be hurt by this, but she had planned the job before she knew that she'd be working for Thompson.

When she arrived in Queensville and found out, she had no intentions of changing her plans. She had felt Thompson out from time to time in seemingly harmless conversations, but she had not—as Clooney suspected—slept with him.

From talking with Thompson she knew he'd never go for robbing his own place, but she also knew that he'd probably come after them.

Then there was the death of Bob Crays. How that had happened she didn't know. If Clooney was right and none of his men did it, then Crays was already dead when they broke in. Somebody else had killed him. Who? Merchant? Thompson? Did they have a falling-out of some kind?

Maybe Clooney was right. Maybe there was a posse. And maybe they were safer together. Watching the other three men by the campfire with their heads together, though, she thought that maybe it was time to start talking to them. So far her only hold was over Clooney. Maybe she needed to extend it to include the others.

After all, she really had no intentions of splitting this money five ways.

THIRTY-EIGHT

On their first night in Arizona, Clint, Hartman, and Ben Thompson found the robbers' first Arizona campfire.

"I can tell a lot from the makeup of this camp," Clint said as they sat around the fire.

"Like what?" Thompson asked.

"Like when they camp they split into three groups. Clooney and Kate probably sit together, and maybe the other two men they brought into the play."

"And Rawlings sits alone?" Hartman asked.

"That'd be my guess," Clint said. "I talked to Rawlings a bit in Queensville. He strikes me as a loner. He doesn't like people much, and he sure doesn't like women. He seems to get along with Clooney, though."

"Uh-oh," Thompson said.

"What?" Hartman asked.

"Recipe for disaster," Thompson said. "Two friends and a woman."

"You think Rawlings wants Kate?" Hartman asked.

"No," Thompson said, "but I don't think he'll like Clooney's relationship with Kate much—especially if she's running the show."

"Kate's smart," Clint said. "If she's running the show she won't make it obvious. And there's another thing."

"What?" Hartman asked.

"She'll probably start working on the other men at some point, trying to charm them."

"It'll probably work," Hartman said.

"It'll start trouble."

"Why?"

"Because Rawlings doesn't like women," Clint said. "He thinks they're all evil."

"Well," Thompson said, "there have been times I'd agree with him."

"Yeah, but this time it could spell disaster. I mean, he got . . . really deep into it, almost like it was a religious thing. He told me that the devil had not only put the apple in the Garden of Eden, but Eve, as well."

"Whoa," Hartman said, "he sounds a bit fanatical."

"That's the word, exactly. Fanatical."

"He could explode," Thompson said. "If Kate starts playing up to all the men—including him—there's no telling what he'd do."

"That's what I'm thinking," Clint said. "If these five people stay together too long, they might do our job for us."

"Hey," Thompson said, "finding their camp with all five of them dead would suit me just fine."

Clint didn't think that possibility was out of the question.

THIRTY-NINE

It was three nights after Rawlings had talked with Beckett and Harper that he finally approached Clooney with the concerns of the three of them.

Rawlings managed to isolate Clooney from Kate, which was unusual. He didn't stop to think about it, however. He simply took advantage of it.

"What's the problem, Mike?"

"The money for one thing," Rawlings said.

"What about it?"

"When are we going to split it up?"

Clooney peered at his partner.

"Is this you askin', or the others?"

"It's all of us, Dan. We want to know."

"Well, I don't know when."

"You mean Kate hasn't told you when?"

"Kate's not runnin' things here, Mike."

"I think she is."

Clooney closed his hands into fists.

"Okay," Rawlings said, before Clooney could say another word, "how much money did we get? Tell me that."

"We got . . . a lot of money."

"You see?" Rawlings said. "She hasn't even told you how much there is. Do you still say she's not running things?"

"Mike," Clooney said, "you know how I feel about this woman."

"And you know how I feel about women, Dan," Rawlings said, "all women. I don't like having her around all the time."

"Mike," Clooney said, "get used to it. This is permanent."

"Dan," Rawlings said, "wake up. She's only using you."

"Mike . . . you know how I feel about her. Why are you pushing me?"

"Give the others their share, Dan, so they can move on, if they want to."

"And you?" Clooney asked. "Do you want to move on? Break up the partnership?"

"Mark my words, Dan," Rawlings said warningly, "if this partnership breaks up, it won't be because of me."

Rawlings walked away then, leaving Clooney by the fire. That was when he saw Kate standing with Harper by the horses. She had one hand on the back of his neck, stroking it while they spoke. Rawlings turned quickly to see if Clooney was looking, but he wasn't.

He turned and as he watched, Kate suddenly pulled Harper's head down and kissed him. Harper stiffened, but then he wrapped his arms around her and the kiss deepened.

Jezebel, Rawlings thought, the worst of whores. Had she tried the same thing with Beckett? Was she beguiling all the men in camp with her charms? And when would she try him?

When she did try him she was in for a big surprise, and so was Clooney. Rawlings realized now, with a great calm coming over him, that the woman could not hide the whore inside of her. Eventually, Clooney would see what she was, and he wouldn't have to worry about her any longer.

FORTY

Rawlings said nothing about what he saw to the others. Over the course of the next few days he waited for the whore to approach him, but she did not. Either she was not ready to, or she knew that it would be futile.

When they crossed into Mexico, Rawlings decided that the charade would not go on much longer.

"Mexico," Thompson said.

They had just crossed into Mexico and reined their horses in to give them a bit of a rest.

"Been here before?" Thompson asked.

"Not much," Hartman said.

"I have," Clint said. "Many times, but not recently."

"Where do you think they'll go?" Thompson asked.

"There are any number of border towns they could

go to," Clint said, "but my guess would be they'll go further in country before they stop."

"There's four of them," Hartman said "One of them must know the country."

"I'd say so," Clint said. "Especially if they've been on the run before."

"We'd better keep moving," Thompson said.

As they rode along Clint said, "Can I ask you something, Ben?"

"Sure."

"Who hired Kate to work in the Queen of Spades?"

"Not me," Thompson said. "I never met any of the people working there until I arrived. I guess either Merchant or Crays must have."

"Which one did most of the hiring?"

"Well, Crays hired me, and he was the one I usually dealt with."

"Crays."

"What are you thinking?" Hartman asked.

"Oh, I'm just thinking about partners," Clint said. "Any partners I ever knew ended up having a falling-out."

"That's true," Thompson said.

"Maybe that's what happened with Merchant and Crays," Clint said, "and maybe that's what will happen with the men we're chasing, especially with a woman in their midst."

"If Merchant and Crays had a falling-out," Thompson said, "and Merchant killed Crays, why would he hire me as sheriff?"

"Maybe," Hartman said, after a nod from Clint told him to go ahead, "it was to get you out of town."

"Hmm," Thompson said, "well, it did that, didn't it?"

Thompson didn't seem pleased that he might have been manipulated into leaving town.

They rode awhile before Clint dismounted to read sign again.

"Looks like I was right," Clint said. "They're not heading for any of the border towns."

"Good," Thompson said, "the longer they stay on the trail, the more chance there is that they'll end up fighting over the woman."

"I think that's true," Clint said. "Stopping in a town would give the others access to other women."

"I can't believe they'd all fall for Kate's scheming," Hartman said.

"You've been with Kate, Rick," Clint said.

"You've got a point there," Hartman said. "She's real convincing."

"That she is."

"I wouldn't know," Thompson said, drawing looks from both men. "Well, I wouldn't. I made it a rule not to sleep with the help."

"And?" Clint asked.

"And . . . she never approached me."

"Did you approach her?" Hartman asked.

"No."

"Maybe she made it a rule never to sleep with her boss," Clint said, "although, if she was planning to rob the place, I can't believe she wouldn't have tried to get some idea of how honest you were."

"Wait a minute," Thompson said, "we did have a conversation once about honesty."

"And?" Clint asked.

"Well, basically I said I would never consider stealing from myself."

"Which is what you would have been doing if you'd helped rob the Queen of Spades," Hartman said, "even though you only ran the place and didn't own it."

"Exactly," Thompson said.

"And she probably never brought it up again after that conversation."

"She didn't."

"How soon after you got there did you have this conversation?" Clint asked.

"The town's only been open a month or so, and I got there soon after." Thompson was thinking out loud. "She was there when I got there ... we must have talked just a few days later."

"It would seem to me," Clint said, "that she was planning this right from the beginning—maybe even before she got there."

"Now what are you thinking?" Hartman asked.

"I think you know."

"That Merchant might have been in on it from the start, also?"

Thompson took over from there.

"That he might even have hired her for that purpose?" he said.

"All possibilities," Clint said.

"Ones that I'll look into when I get back," Thompson said. "I don't like being played for a sucker."

"Nobody does, Ben," Clint said.

FORTY-ONE

"Why don't we stop in a town?" Beckett asked.

"I'm gettin' tired of your complaints, Beckett," Clooney said.

Beckett, emboldened by the knowledge that Kate actually preferred him to Clooney, said, "Then pay me my share and you won't have to deal with me anymore."

They were across the fire from each other, and Beckett was cooking again. Now he dropped the pan onto the fire and stood up.

"And I'll tell you somethin' else," he said. "I ain't cookin' anymore."

Clooney stood up.

"As long as you're ridin' with me, you'll do what you're told."

"Well," Beckett said, "pay me off and—"

"Why don't you two shut up?" Harper said.

161

"What?" Clooney said.

"You shut up," Beckett said.

Given more courage by the hot looks Kate was sending his way, and the memory of her kisses on his lips, Harper said, "Watch your mouth, Beckett. I'm tired of hearing you, too."

"Oh, yeah?"

"The two of you shut up," Clooney said. "What the hell is wrong with you?"

Off to the side Kate watched as all the seeds she had been sewing over the past few days were starting to bloom.

Mike Rawlings also watched. This was what he was waiting for. The other three men were just inches from being at each other's throats, they just needed one last little push.

"You do the cooking," Beckett was saying to Clooney.

"I don't cook," Clooney said.

"Oh, no, that's right, you're the big leader. You don't even know how much money we got from the casino, that's how much of a leader you are."

"And you do?"

"Yeah, I do know," Beckett said.

"How do you know?"

"Kate told me."

"You been talkin' to Kate?"

"I been doing more than talkin' to her," Beckett said.

"Hey," Harper said, pointing at Beckett, "watch what you say about Kate."

"What the hell are you guys talkin' about?" Clooney

demanded. "Neither of you has been near Kate. She's my woman."

"You think so?" Beckett asked. "Maybe she prefers somebody else."

"Maybe she does," Harper said to Beckett. "Me!"

"You? She prefers me!"

Suddenly Harper lunged at Beckett across the fire, sending the frying pan flying. The two men rolled into the dirt, locked together. Clooney, shocked at what was going on, rushed to them and tried to separate them, and suddenly somebody's gun was out and it went off. The sounds of a slug striking flesh and somebody grunting came in quick succession, and then suddenly there was another shot, but not from any of their three guns.

The three men froze and looked around. They saw Mike Rawlings standing with his gun smoking. He was standing over Kate McElroy. Kate was lying on her side on the ground with a hole in her forehead, just a touch of blood oozing from the wound. Rawlings put his foot on her shoulder and rolled her over onto her back.

"What—" Clooney said.

"Hey—" Beckett said.

"Shit," Harper said, because he was the one who was hit—and it was by a bullet from his own gun.

"You son of a—" Beckett said, going for his gun.

Rawlings didn't hesitate. He snapped one shot off at Beckett, catching the man square in the chest. Beckett staggered back, tripped over Harper's prone figure, and fell on top of him.

"Shit!" Harper said again.

"Anybody else want to try?" Rawlings asked.

Clooney stared at him, then looked at Kate.

"Wha—what did you do that for?" he demanded.

"Look at yourselves," Rawlings said. "She has you fighting among yourselves. She was hoping you'd kill each other."

"That's crazy!" Clooney said.

"Crazy?" Rawlings asked. "Tell him, Harper."

"T-tell him what?" Harper said, holding his hand to his side. He was unsuccessfully trying to staunch the flow of blood from his wound.

"Tell him about Kate sniffing around you."

Clooney looked at Harper.

"What about it?"

"I need help—"

"Answer the question!" Clooney said.

"Y-yeah, it's true," Harper said. "She started comin' around me a couple of days ago. Said I was the man she wanted to be with."

"I saw her kissing him," Rawlings said, "and Beckett, too."

"Beckett, too?"

"That's right," Rawlings said. "The only one she didn't come around was me, because she knew I'd resist her. Face it, Dan. She was a whore. She was going to try to get all the money for herself."

Clooney walked to Kate's body and stared down at her.

"I'll bet she's got a gun in the saddlebags with the money," Rawlings said.

Clooney bent over and pulled the saddlebags free of Kate's grasp. When she died her hand had closed on it, and he had to yank it to get it away from her. He opened it and found the Navy Colt.

"See?" Rawlings said.

"Jesus," Harper said, "I'm bleedin' to death." He looked up at Rawlings and Clooney and said, "You gotta help me."

Clooney walked to him, pointed the Navy Colt, and said, "I'll help you."

"Hey, wait—"

Clooney put a bullet in Harper's forehead, just like Rawlings did to Kate.

He turned and faced Rawlings, who still had his gun out. They stared at each other for a few moments, and then Clooney tossed the Navy Colt into the dirt.

"Two-way split?" he said to Rawlings.

Rawlings spread his hands and said, "That's all I've ever wanted, Dan."

Clooney nodded, walked to Kate's body, and kicked it once.

"Let's not even bury them," he said. "None of them deserve it."

FORTY-TWO

Clint, Hartman, and Thompson all heard the shot and stood up. They stood around the campfire listening, and heard the second shot.

"What the hell—" Thompson said.

"Shhh," Clint said.

They waited and heard the third shot, then waited some more, until there was one more shot. Then nothing.

"What's going on?" Hartman wondered aloud.

"I think maybe push finally came to shove," Clint said quietly.

"You mean you think they finally had a falling-out?" Thompson asked.

"Probably," Clint said. "It was bound to happen. There's nothing we can do about it now, though. We'll just have to wait until morning to find out."

166

"Least we know we're within range of them," Hartman said.

"Yes," Clint said, "Kate was slowing them down."

"Maybe tomorrow," Thompson said, "she won't be slowing them down anymore."

FORTY-THREE

They got an early start in the morning and before noon they came upon the robbers' campsite.

"Jesus," Hartman said, "looks like they really went at it."

They reined in their horses and dismounted. Each of them walked to a body to check it. Clint walked over to Kate's.

"She's dead," he called out. "Shot in the forehead."

"This one, too," Hartman said. "He's hit twice, once in the forehead."

"This one's shot in the heart," Thompson said.

They gathered around the cold fire.

"It's got to be they fought over the woman, and Clooney and Rawlings got the best of it," Clint said.

"Now they have the money and only have to do a two-way split," Thompson said.

"Poor Kate," Clint said.

"I guess we'll never know now if she was working with Merchant or not," Hartman said.

"Or whether Merchant is crooked or not," Thompson said.

"You can bluff him when you get back," Clint said to Thompson.

"You mean lie to him?"

"Sure," Clint said, "tell him Kate gave him up just before she died, and see what happens."

"Good idea," Thompson said, "but I'm not going back just yet, not until I get that money."

"They're still heading south," Clint said. "My guess is they'll stop somewhere before dark."

"Well, let's get after them," Thompson said. "They don't have Kate to slow them down anymore."

As they went to mount up, Hartman noticed that his horse was limping.

"He's lame," he said, after examining the horse's leg and hoof.

"Can't ride double," Thompson said. "It'll slow us down too much."

"He can ride with me," Clint said, "and you can go on ahead, Ben."

"No," Hartman said. "Why don't I just stay behind and bury these people. After that I'll look around for one of their horses."

"That's a good idea," Clint said. "From the tracks Clooney and Rawlings didn't take any of the horses with them, so they must be around here somewhere."

"Okay, then," Hartman said. "I'll catch up to you, and meet you somewhere along the way."

"You got enough water?" Clint asked.

"Half a canteen."

Clint took his canteen from his saddle and tossed it to Hartman.

"I'll get some more along the way."

"Thanks."

"Let's get moving," Thompson said. He looked at Hartman and said, "See you later, Rick."

"Good luck," Hartman said.

Before they left, Clint looked down at Kate's body again and shook his head.

"Don't feel too sorry for her," Thompson said. "She made her choice."

"I know," Clint said, "but it's still such a waste."

A few hours ahead Rawlings and Clooney reined in.

"You know, if there's a posse after us, they heard those shots last night," Clooney said.

"Ain't no posse gonna follow us into Mexico," Rawlings said.

"Ben Thompson will."

"Don't matter," Rawlings said. "He's only one man."

"Yeah, right."

"Dan, you okay?"

Clooney looked at Rawlings, and then nodded.

"She got under my skin, Mike."

"I know," Rawlings said. "But that don't happen with whores. At least with whores, you *know* they're whores, doin' what they're doin' for money."

"You know what?" Clooney said. "You're absolutely right. From now on, I'm with you. Let's get us some of those Mexican whores."

Rawlings laughed and said, "Now you're talkin'."

FORTY-FOUR

The Mexican town of Santa Luz was used to playing host to American desperados—at least, those that did not want to hide out in the border towns.

When Mike Rawlings and Dan Clooney rode into town everyone knew who they were and what they were. They also knew there was a good chance that the two Americans had brought a lot of money with them.

Once upon a time there were men in Santa Luz who would try to steal money from visiting American bandits, but the town fathers put a stop to that. They wanted the rich American thieves to come to Santa Luz and spend their money. If word got out that Americans were being robbed, that would not happen.

Clooney had been to Santa Luz before and knew that he and Rawlings would be welcomed with open arms, as long as they spent money.

Soon after they arrived and left their horses at the livery, they appeared at the cantina and ordered a huge meal.

"And after the meal," Rawlings told the cantina's owner, "we want whores."

"*Sí*, señor," the man said, "the finest whores in all Mexico."

"You hear that, Dan?" Rawlings asked. "Not just any whores, but the finest whores in all Me-hi-co!"

"I heard," Clooney said, "but after the tortillas, huh?"

"*Mas* tortillas!" Rawlings shouted.

Clooney and Rawlings ate lots of tortillas, lots of rice, and drank lots of beer and whiskey. When they were done there were four whores there for their pleasure, and rooms in the back.

Rawlings took two whores to one room, while Clooney took two to another room, along with the saddlebags of money. In the room it occurred to him that they still had not counted the money in the bags. In fact, he had not even looked in the bags since Rawlings killed Kate. He'd only stuck his hand in and took out the Navy Colt.

He sat on the rickety bed while the two whores undressed, watching them as their big breasts and butts came into view. He pulled out a handful of money— only it wasn't money, it was newspaper cut roughly into the shape of money.

"What the—"

The two whores came to press him between them and he pushed them away violently. They fell to the floor with displeased groans as Clooney upended the saddlebags and dumped the contents onto the bed.

Lots and lots of cash-sized newspaper, and no money.
"That bitch!"

Rawlings was already in bed with the two whores.
His hands were playing with the breasts of one while
his mouth was full of the breast of another when Clooney kicked the door in.

"What the hell—" Rawlings said. He sat up and saw
Clooney standing in the doorway. "What's the matter,
Dan, you wanna switch whores?"

"That bitch!" Clooney said, for the second time in
sixty seconds.

"What are you—"

"There's no money."

"What?" Rawlings sat straight up, not sure he'd
heard correctly. "Get off me!" he snapped at the
whores.

Clooney walked to the bed and dumped the contents
of the saddlebags again. It was still all newspaper.

"Jesus," Rawlings said, picking up handfuls of the
stuff, "when did she have time to do this?"

"There was cash in those saddlebags when we left
Queensville, Mike," Clooney said, "I saw it."

"But you never counted it, did you?" Rawlings
asked. "And you never got another look at it the whole
time we were traveling. You let her keep it from you."

"But—but what did she do with it?"

Rawlings threw the newspaper on the floor and told
the whores, "Get out!"

They wanted to be paid, but Rawlings shouted at them
again and they ran out. Clooney slammed the door.

"When did she have time—"

"It had to be while we were camped and asleep," Rawlings said. "Jesus, she must have done it right under the nose of whoever was on watch."

"Not on mine," Clooney said.

"Or mine," Rawlings said. "It must have been Beckett or Harper."

"Maybe they were even in on it," Clooney said. "But what did she do with it?"

"On the trail somewhere," Rawlings said, "hidden or buried. It's got to be."

Just then there was a knock on the door.

"Go away!" Rawlings said.

"But, señors," the owner called, "you have not paid for the food, or the *putas*."

"We didn't use the whores," Rawlings shouted, "and the food was lousy."

"B-but, señors, the *cerveza*—"

"The beer was bad, too," Clooney shouted.

"Señor," the man said, pounding on the door, "you must pay—"

"Shit," Rawlings said. He grabbed his gun from the holster hanging on the bedpost and fired four shots into the thin door. From behind it they heard the sound of a body slumping to the floor.

"Paid in full, goddamn it!" Rawlings shouted.

FORTY-FIVE

When Clint and Thompson rode into the town of
Santa Luz there was some commotion going on. The
main street was choked with people who were shouting
in Spanish.

"Do you understand them?" Clint asked Thompson.

"No," Thompson said, "but they're upset about
something."

"Yeah," Clint said, "and they're not looking at us
too happily either."

As they moved further down the street the crowd sep-
arated to allow them to pass, but then closed again behind them. Soon they realized they were surrounded by
angry Mexicans who were not looking at them kindly.

Finally, ahead of them they saw what the commotion
was all about.

It was a hanging, and being hanged were Dan Clooney and Mike Rawlings.

"Adams!" Rawlings shouted when he recognized him. "Adams, you gotta help us."

Both men had their hands tied behind them, and their hats and gun belts removed. They were standing on a buckboard, and two ropes had been strung down from the beam of the building that stuck out over the street.

As Rawlings began shouting, the townspeople settled down and stared at Clint and Thompson.

A man stepped forward, wearing a badge, and looked up at them.

"Señors, these are your friends?" the man asked.

"Who are you?" Thompson asked.

"I am *el jefe* here," the man said. "How do you say? The sheriff."

"I'm the sheriff of Queensville, Nevada," Thompson said, hoping that no one would ask for his badge. "These men are not friends, they are fugitives. I am hunting them."

"You have found them, señor," the sheriff said, "but you cannot take them back."

"Why not?"

"They have killed a man," the sheriff said. "A simple man who was only demanding to be paid for the food and . . . comfort he provided. For this he was shot down like a dog."

"Adams, please!" Rawlings shouted.

"Why didn't you pay the man, Rawlings?" Clint asked. "You've got plenty of money."

"We have no money!" Rawlings said.

"What?" Thompson said. "Where's the money you stole?"

"Gone," Rawlings said. "That bitch Kate hid it somewhere."

"All we got was some cut up newspaper," Clooney added. "Come on, Thompson, Adams, you gotta get us out of here."

"These men are to come back to the United States with me, where they will be hung after a trial," Thompson said.

"Señor," the sheriff said, "it would be much simpler for them to be hung here, without a trial, no?"

"Sheriff—"

"Señor," the sheriff said, "look around you. These people want a hanging, and they don't care who gets hung, eh? *Comprende?*"

Clint and Thompson looked around, and they understood. If they tried to stop this hanging, they just might join the party.

Thompson looked at Clint and said, "If there's no money, then we're done here."

Clint looked around and had no choice but to agree.

"Let's go," Thompson said. "Adios, Sheriff."

"Adios, señor."

The crowd moved just enough for Clint and Thompson to turn their horses so they could ride back out of town. Behind them they heard the screams of Rawlings and Clooney to help them, but neither man had the urge to face down a whole town on their behalf.

"Adams!" Rawlings shouted.

"Thompson!" Clooney called.

As they reached the edge of town there was a sudden shout from the crowd, and suddenly they couldn't hear the two Americans anymore.

FORTY-SIX

"It bothers you, doesn't it?" Thompson asked later.

"What?" Clint asked.

"Leaving them there, to be hung?"

"It might bother me more if Kate were still alive," Clint said.

"I know what you mean," Thompson said.

Suddenly they became aware of a rider up ahead coming toward them and they reined in, ready to draw their guns if they were faced with *bandidos* or a Spanish patrol. Instead, it was Rick Hartman, riding a horse they hadn't seen before.

"What are you fellas doing here?" he asked.

"We're finished," Thompson said. "Headin' back to the States."

"Where are Rawlings and Clooney?"

"Dead," Clint said.

"You killed them?"

Clint shook his head.

"Somebody took care of that for us."

Quickly, Clint explained what fate had befallen the two Americans in the town of Santa Luz.

"Too bad," Hartman said.

"What we have to do now," Thompson said, "is find the money."

"No," Hartman said, "we don't."

He reached into a saddlebag and brought out two stacks of bills.

"Where'd you find it?" Clint asked.

"I was looking for one of the horses and found it where Kate must have hidden it, among some rocks. She must have had cut up newspaper in one saddlebag and the cash in the other. After she hid the cash, she spread the newspaper out into the two saddlebags."

"And none of those men ever wanted to see the cash," Thompson said, shaking his head.

"She was a persuasive woman," Clint said. "What I can't understand is how she expected to get away with it. Sooner or later they would have found out."

"Maybe," Thompson suggested, "she planned to get down to one man, and she would have told him where the money was."

"If she wanted to split it with him," Clint said. "When it got down to one man, maybe she would have taken care of him, too."

"She was some woman," Hartman said, putting the cash back.

"I'll take that money back to Queensville," Thompson said.

''Be my guest,'' Hartman said, tossing the saddlebags to Thompson, who caught them neatly.

''Did you count it?'' Thompson asked.

''Oh, yeah.''

''How much?''

''Fifty thousand.''

Clint and Thompson both whistled.

''Worth killing for,'' Thompson said.

''But not worth dying for,'' Clint said.

''You fellas want to come back with me when we get to the States?''

''I don't think so,'' Clint said. ''We'll ride east a ways until we can cross back into the States in Texas.''

''Suit yourselves,'' Thompson said. ''I appreciate you comin' along this far, though.''

''What are you going to do about Merchant?'' Clint asked.

''Like you said, I'll bluff him. Maybe he was in on it, maybe he wasn't. I guess I'll have to decide for myself, if he doesn't confess.''

''Maybe he'll get away with it,'' Hartman said.

''Even if he does,'' Thompson said, ''how long do you think a town like that will last? When the two-bit gamblers and con artists start comin' in, it'll be the beginning of the end.''

''If you figured that,'' Clint asked, ''why'd you take the job?''

Thompson shrugged and said, ''It was somethin' to do for a while.''

''Let's get out of Mexico,'' Clint said, ''before the people from that town figure out that this money has to be somewhere.''

"Clint," Thompson said, "we haven't gotten along in the past, and we probably won't in the future, but thanks."

They shook hands, and Thompson and Hartman exchanged a wave. After that, they rode in their separate directions.

"Do me a favor?" Hartman said as he and Clint rode off together.

"What?"

"In the future," Hartman said, "just leave me to my place. Don't entice me to go on any trips with you, huh?"

"Why would I?" Clint asked. "You've been nothing but bad luck on this one."

Hartman opened his mouth, but Clint spurred Duke on ahead before the drawn out, "Whaaa—?" could come out.

Watch for

CHINATOWN ASSASSIN

180th novel in the exciting GUNSMITH series
from Jove

Coming in December!

A special offer for people who enjoy
reading the best Westerns published today.

WESTERNS!

NO OBLIGATION

Mail the coupon below

To start your subscription and
receive 2 FREE WESTERNS, fill
out the coupon below and mail it
today. We'll send your first shipment which includes 2 FREE
BOOKS as soon as we receive it.

Mail To: **True Value Home Subscription Services, Inc. P.O. Box 5235**
120 Brighton Road, Clifton, New Jersey 07015-5235

YES! I want to start reviewing the very best Westerns being published today. Send me my first
shipment of 6 Westerns for me to preview FREE for 10 days. If I decide to keep them, I'll pay for
just 4 of the books at the low subscriber price of $2.75 each; a total $11.00 (a $21.00 value). Then
each month I'll receive the 6 newest and best Westerns to preview Free for 10 days. If I'm not satisfied I may return them within 10 days and owe nothing. Otherwise I'll be billed at the special low
subscriber rate of $2.75 each; a total of $16.50 (at least a $21.00 value) and save $4.50 off the
publishers price. There are never any shipping, handling or other hidden charges. I understand I
am under no obligation to purchase any number of books and I can cancel my subscription at any
time, no questions asked. In any case the 2 FREE books are mine to keep.

Name _____

Street Address _____ Apt. No. _____

City _____ State _____ Zip Code _____

Telephone _____

Signature _____
(if under 18 parent or guardian must sign)

Terms and prices subject to change. Orders subject
to acceptance by True Value Home Subscription
Services, Inc.

11969-5

J. R. ROBERTS

THE
GUNSMITH